The Wizard's Daughter

D1598428

Also by Jeff Minerd

The Sky Riders of Etherium
The Sailweaver's Son
The Wizard's Daughter

THE SKY RIDERS OF ETHERIUM

The Wizard's Daughter

By

Jeff Minerd

HOLLISTON, MASSACHUSETTS

THE WIZARD'S DAUGHTER
Copyright © 2018 by Jeff Minerd

Cover Art by Silviya Yordanova.

First printing September 2018
10 9 8 7 6 5 4 3 2 1

ISBN # 978-1-60975-227-9
ISBN (eBook) # 978-1-60975-228-6
LCCN # 2018946435

Silver Leaf Books, LLC
P.O. Box 6460
Holliston, MA 01746
+1-888-823-6450

Visit our web site at www.SilverLeafBooks.com

To my parents,
Timothy and Geraldine Minerd.

Acknowledgements

A lot of people helped me with *The Wizard's Daughter,* and I'm grateful.

Thanks to Kathy Salecki for her support and advice, including pointing out the book needed an epilogue to balance the prologue I'd written. (I'd totally missed that!) Thanks to my sister, Laura Minerd-Ruffino, and my parents Geraldine and Timothy Minerd, who in addition to being tireless supporters and volunteer publicists also gave me helpful feedback. Thanks to my brother-in-law Chuck Ruffino for this thoughtful and sometimes humorous comments. My writer friends Nora Bradbury-Haehl and Christine Adamo also gave me valuable suggestions and advice, as did Melody Russo. Finally, a special thanks to Debi Mansour. She read an early draft, and over the course of several conversations she helped me improve key elements and scenes and make this a much better book.

BURNING MOUNTAINS

DRAGONLORD'S REALM

KAIDO

ONSHU

KYO→

KOKU

USHU

EASTERN KINGDOMS

NO-MAN'S CRAG

WIND'S TEETH

EASTERN

HIGHSPIRE MOUNTAINS

DRAGONSBACK MOUNTAINS

OCEAN OF CLOUD

KINGDOM OF SPIRE

The
Wizard's
Daughter

PROLOGUE

It was a lookout, of course, who saw them first.

"Dragons!" he called from his position atop the main-mast. "Three of 'em. Two points off the starboard bow. Elevation near ten thousand feet."

There was a flurry of activity aboard the huge airship. An alarm bell clanged. Officers shouted orders. Men scrambled up into the rigging to adjust the enormous, wing-like sails in case the captain called for a course change. On the main deck, gun crews assembled at the bronze cannons whose gleaming barrels pointed out at the sky. Below decks, the cannoneers threw open the gun ports and with a noisy rumble ran out the guns. Everywhere, men took up positions with buckets of sand at the ready, prepared to smother drag-onfire if necessary.

Admiral Adamus Strake, head of the royal fleet and captain of the flagship *Dragonbane*, stood at a command deck rail and studied the creatures through his spyglass. A large female, flanked by two smaller males. This far north, and with fall's chilly bite in the wind, he'd expected them to be polar dragons, heading for their wintering grounds further south. But these dragons had the bright red scales and glittering golden bellies of dragons from the east, from someplace where the mountains spewed fire and ash. What could they be doing so far from home? And where were they going? Strake gauged their direction, using the far-off tips of the mountains of Frost as a reference point among all the clouds and empty sky. He checked his compass. If the dragons remained on their current course, they would reach the Highspire Mountains in a few days.

That was bad.

The Highspire Mountains were home, the main mountain chain in the Kingdom of Spire. More than two hundred and fifty thousand souls lived there, most in small villages with no defense against a dragon attack. Even the capital city of Selestria, with its castle and high stone walls and constant roving guard of battleships like the *Dragonbane*, could suffer serious casualties at the hands of three dragons. Especially if taken by surprise, at night, as dragons tended to do.

"Shall we engage 'em, admiral?" asked Strake's first lieutenant, a tall woman with close-cropped blonde hair. She stood at his side, squinting at the creatures through her own spyglass.

Strake's weather-beaten face, crisscrossed and pockmarked with old burn scars, took on a solemn expression. He sighed. "I guess we'll have to."

Unlike his predecessor, the notorious Admiral Scud, Strake took no pleasure in killing dragons. He always thrilled to see them. They were such beautiful creatures, so perfectly formed. Ultimate predators. The perfect flying and fighting machines. Still, you couldn't allow the beasts to fly into populated areas, if you could help it. A single stray dragon could level a village and eat all its livestock in the time it took most people to finish their breakfast. That's why battleships of the royal fleet spent so much time on dragon patrols.

Another reason Strake didn't want to engage the dragons was his diplomatic mission to the Kingdom of Frost in the north. A dragon fight would mar the looks of his ship. First impressions were important on diplomatic missions, Strake knew. He wanted to project an image of wealth and strength. He'd had the ship scrubbed and polished from top to bottom. The magnificent *Dragonbane* with its five tall masts and acres of billowing silvery sails would look much less impressive if it were to come limping up to the capital city of Frost with its sails in tatters and all its polished wood scratched and scorched. Still, there was no avoiding it.

"Prepare for action!" Strake bellowed. "Fire up the props and accelerate to attack speed!" His voice carried clearly from the bow to the stern to the tip of the tallest mast.

In the belly of the airship, engineers cranked open throttle valves that channeled streams of fresh fuel to the boilers. The ship had been recently modified to use the new fuel, a flammable gas, instead of coal. The four massive propellers at the ship's stern churned as it accelerated. Steam billowed from vents on the underside.

A small, four-man messenger ship was launched from the deck. The men on that ship had orders to carry news of the dragon sighting back to airfleet headquarters on Selemont.

"Straight at 'em!" Strake ordered. This was the standard tactic for fighting dragons. The creatures would respond to the maneuver as they would to a challenge from another dragon or large flying creature—by flying straight at the ship in return, aiming for the carved dragon figurehead at the bow. The typical dragon of Etherium was about as smart as a bear, and they attacked as a bear would attack. Or, to be more accurate, they attacked as an insane homicidal bear with unresolved anger issues would attack—hurling themselves maniacally through the air, talons outstretched seeking blood, jaws gaping and roaring, spitting malevolence and fire—and then biting and burning, ripping and rending, and thoroughly squashing and smashing every living and non-living thing within reach.

The red dragons with the golden bellies turned and flew straight at the battleship as expected. The large female in the lead, a male off each wingtip. However, very shortly, these dragons were about to do something completely unexpected. A number of things, actually.

When the battleship closed to within two-hundred yards of the creatures, Strake ordered the ship hard about to port. The steeringman spun the wheel, the massive rudder turned, the fluttering sails were angled and trimmed, and the ship turned sharply to port, presenting the cannons all along its starboard side to the trio of dragons. Royal cannoneers train and train again until they are able to hit a dragon on the fly at two hundred yards as easily as most people can spit and hit their own shoe.

"Fire!" Strake shouted.

As one, the cannons flashed and roared, spewing huge clouds of smoke and bucking backward. The ship shuddered, beams creaking with strain.

And the strangest thing happened.

The moment the cannons flashed, the dragons dodged and dispersed, scattering evasively. The shots passed through empty space where dragon flesh had been only a split-second before.

Strake blinked, stunned. Unsure he'd seen what he'd actually seen.

The dragons had dodged at exactly the right moment. The cannoneers had missed.

Royal cannoneers rarely miss.

Dragons don't dodge like that.

And now something even stranger was happening. Instead of regrouping, the dragons split up. One flew at the ship from the portside. Another came at them to starboard. And a third, one of the males, took off after the messenger ship. After the messenger ship! Dragons never attacked messenger ships. They were too small to be perceived as a threat. Strake gripped the command deck rail with white knuckles. The men in the messenger ship, the men he'd ordered there, stood no chance against a dragon attack.

The cannoneers were so flabbergasted by their misses and the dragons' odd behavior that several crews forgot to reload until Strake shouted the order. There was nothing he could do about the messenger ship. He needed to concentrate on saving his own ship now. To his dismay, the dragons were no longer flying straight at him. They spiraled and zagged erratically, trying to evade more cannon shot. Strake's mind raced. If these dragons were somehow intelligent enough to avoid cannons—to know to dodge in that split-second between the cannon flash and the arrival of the ball, to know to zig and zag as they approached—then his cannoneers could no longer fire in unison. The shots needed to be less predictable.

"Do not fire together!" he ordered. "Fire at will!"

And by wind and weather, hit something this time, his mind added.

The cannons cracked like thunder. The sound of each shot rang in Strake's ears. The ship shuddered, bobbed, and rolled on the wind. The sails chattered.

They got one! The male approaching from portside. A shot straight through the heart. There was a spray of blood, and his wings crumpled and folded. He fell spinning toward the blanket of clouds that covered the surface of Etherium far below.

Several shots from the starboard batteries pierced the wings of the female dragon as she approached. But the small clean holes they made in the webbing of her wings barely slowed her down. When she was fifty yards from the ship— and the cannoneers furiously reloading—she dove.

And disappeared.

"Where did she go?" men shouted to each other. "Where is she?" "Do you see her?"

Men rushed to the rails and looked over the side. The sky above and below was empty.

"Where in blazes is she?" Strake yelled. But he was afraid

he knew the answer.

The ship's steering wheel gave a sudden spin, sending the steeringman sprawling to the deck. From underneath the ship, there came the sound of wood being splintered by massive jaws.

Men shouted from the aft deck railing. "The rudder! She's chewing the rudder!"

"She's underneath the ship!" the first lieutenant shouted, bewildered. The stern dipped as if a heavy weight had attached itself to the rear of the ship. Strake could imagine the dragon, anchored upside down to the belly of his ship by her talons, attacking the rudder. More sounds of wood being rent and torn. The ship's steering wheel spun loosely.

"She's taken out our steering," the first lieutenant gasped. "We're dead in the air."

Strake strode to the wheel and gave it an experimental turn. He could feel there was no longer any rudder attached below. It boggled the mind! One's rudder was of course a prime target when battling another ship. Losing it meant you could no longer steer, were at the mercy of the currents and your enemy. But for a dragon to take out a rudder? They didn't know how to do that. Their animal minds couldn't conceive of doing something like that! Strake couldn't have been any more astounded if the dragon had landed on his deck and politely challenged him to a game of chess.

"Crossbows, spears, and shields, all hands!" Strake shouted. "We'll be at close quarters soon!"

Men scrambled to tie up the cannons. Some grabbed up spears and fire-resistant shields from racks. Others furiously cocked and loaded crossbows.

With a frenzied whooshing of wings, the dragon flipped herself from underneath the ship onto the command deck. She was larger and heavier than an elephant. She spread her wings and roared. The ship lurched and rolled. To their credit, the airmen aboard the *Dragonbane* kept their feet. Strake could smell the dragon's breath now, a horrible acrid smell that watered the eyes. He shouted for his men to aim at the eyes of the beast, but he had little hope for his ship or his men now. Once you let a dragon get onto the deck of your ship, you were as good as toast. Your cannons were useless. You had only toys to fight with.

And the dragon had fire.

The men fired crossbows and hurled spears. Most bounced off the dragon's armored scales. A few hit and stuck, but to no effect. One crossbow bolt stuck in the corner of the dragon's left eye, but at a shallow angle, not deep enough to reach the brain. Only enough to make her roar even more furiously. Her chest swelled with a huge breath. In one convulsive movement, she clamped down her mouth, striking sparks with her teeth, and expelled an awful-smelling, viscous, flammable fluid through her clenched teeth and nostrils. It became a spray of sticky fire.

Gobbets of fire flew and stuck everywhere—to the deck, to the masts, to the crew. Men rolled on the deck to extinguish themselves. Others heaved buckets of sand to smother the flames. Men tripped and fell over each other. They scrabbled over the pitching deck trying to retrieve dropped weapons. The dragon spewed fire again, then lashed out with her tail and talons, and what little order remained aboard the ship gave way to mayhem and madness. There was nothing but screams and smoke, the tearing of wood and flesh. The dragon's jaws dripped slime and flame. Strake drew his sword and charged through the confusion, straight at the dragon, calling for his men to join him. The beast's armored tail smacked him in the head and sent him skidding across the deck.

He had one thought before losing consciousness.

No! Please! Not again…

* * *

When Strake awoke, he found himself staring into the murderous eyes of a dragon. Each eye was the size of a bowling ball, the irises a dazzling gold flecked with green, the black pupils vertical slits that opened onto a nightmare. The dragon's face was a few feet from his. It was the female. The male's face hovered nearby. They stank. Strake squirmed, and found he was bound from chest to knees by the tight grip of a dragon's talons. He couldn't move at all. He could just breathe…if he inhaled shallowly.

He craned his head around. The dragons were perched on the deck of his ship. What he could see of it was blackened and smoldering. He didn't see any living men. He could only hope some had escaped by parachute. Sky rider parachutes are cunningly built. In the buoyant atmosphere of Etherium, they can keep a man aloft indefinitely. And they're equipped with toggles for steering.

None of your men escaped. My dragons saw to that. I'm terribly sorry.

Strake heard the voice inside his head. But somehow it seemed to be coming from the dragon's eyes.

I had to reward them for the work they'd done. And let them sate their anger for the one you killed. And they so love human flesh. You know how it is with dragons.

Strake blinked. It was said that some dragons could communicate with each other telepathically. But he'd never heard of dragons communicating with humans in this way. And he'd certainly never heard of dragons being able to channel the telepathic speech of a human, which is what seemed to be happening now.

"Who are you?" he asked.

*Come meet me…*the voice said, and the dragons leapt into the air.

ONE

Brieze's mother was acting strange. She'd been moping and sighing around the wizard's house all day, doing dumb things. She'd left her hairbrush on the *stairs* of all places, where Brieze had nearly tripped over it and broken her neck, and she'd forgotten to feed the wizard's exotic birds, which squawked hungrily from their cages in the parlor. Brieze was pretty sure her mother's state of mind had something to do with Tobias the handyman. The two had stopped talking to each other, and Tobias was moping around the house too.

Her mother had wandered outside to the wide front lawn that stretched to the edge of the wizard's floating island. Brieze kept an eye on her from an upstairs window as she played chess with the wizard. The wizard took a long time making his moves, and she went to the window and watched while she waited.

Now her mother was doing *more* dumb things. She wasn't wearing a cloak, even though the fall chill outside hinted strongly of the winter to come, and she was standing much too close to the island's edge, especially for such a windy day. And it was hard for Brieze to tell at this distance, but she didn't seem to be wearing a parachute pack, which was not just dumb but *dangerous*.

With the late afternoon sun low in the sky and the island positioned near the Highspire Mountains, the view was spectacular. From horizon to horizon, silvery gray clouds blanketed the surface of Etherium, as they always did. To the east, the mountains rose tall and craggy and green out of these clouds, reaching for the sky. The mountain range stretched northward and southward in lazy zigs and zags, the farthest mountains fading off into the distance. The sky was a pretty shade of pinkish-purple. Banks of cumulus clouds piled high on the horizon like echoes of the mountains.

The nearest mountain was so close that, if her mother were looking at the view, she could have made out the terraced fields and orchards on its lower flanks. She could have glimpsed the tiny specks of ox- and donkey-drawn carts making their way along the roads that spiraled or switchbacked up the mountainside. Further up the mountain, she could have seen the city of Selestria in all its sunlit splendor, the brightly-colored pennants flying from the roofs of the stone houses, the airships swarming about the city like busy bees—constantly touching down and taking off—their silvery sails glinting when they caught the sun. At the mountain's crown, she could have admired Castle Selestria, which seemed as much a part of the sky as part of the earth, its tallest towers and turrets lost in the clouds.

But Brieze's mother wasn't looking at any of this. She hadn't gone outside for the view. She stood with her head down, shoulders hunched, and her hands thrust deep into her pockets, muttering to herself. She didn't notice the gusts of wind tugging at her skirt. The knotted bun of her hair had come undone—it whipped around her face in a frenzy.

Brieze unclipped a brand-new spyglass from the belt of her black flightsuit. It had been a gift from the wizard for her sixteenth birthday. She studied her mother through it. The house's rafters groaned in the wind.

"Ah ha!" the wizard said, and advanced one of his pawns with a satisfied little clink. "Your move."

"She's not wearing a parachute," Brieze said, peering through the spyglass.

"Hmmmm…?" the wizard looked up from the chessboard, his blue eyes blinking beneath bushy white brows.

"It's windy out there and she forgot to grab a chute from the porch."

The wizard came to the window. He frowned at the distant figure of Patentia Crofter standing near the island's edge with her shoulders hunched against the wind, her hands in her pockets, her hair flying. "That is exceedingly dangerous," he said, his brow furrowing and his eyebrows squinching closer together.

And, as if to prove him right, a huge gust of wind ballooned Patentia's skirt, lifted her off her feet, and carried her tumbling end-over-end off the island's edge.

Brieze screamed.

The wizard dashed from the room, knocking over the chessboard. The pieces scattered across the floor. He shouted at the top of his lungs, "Overside! Someone's gone overside!" His footsteps thumped down the hallway toward the stairs. People had been windswept off the island before. It was an accepted risk of island life. The islanders would form a rescue party. They would pull on parachutes, launch airships, toss lifelines over the side. But by the time they did any of this, it might be too late. Things, including people, fall slowly in the thick atmosphere of Etherium. But they do fall, and they gather speed as they go.

So Brieze didn't waste time with the three flights of stairs.

She threw open the window, checked her flightsuit, and jumped out—headfirst.

She spread her arms wide. The loose folds of fabric between her wrists and waist snapped taut in the wind and became wings. The wind tried to whisk her away, but she wrestled with it, steered into it and used the weight of her body to bring herself down to the ground in a long, wobbling arc. She hit the green lawn in front of the wizard's house shoulder first and rolled to her feet. Dizzy, she dashed to the porch, where dozens of parachute packs were stacked neatly by the double front doors.

She grabbed up a pack and slung it around her shoulders. There was commotion inside the house—confused shouting, running footsteps. Soon, she knew, people would come spilling out of the house onto the porch to form the rescue party. If she waited, she could lead them to the spot where her mother had gone over, which might increase the chances of a rescue.

But Brieze couldn't waste her precious head start. She pelted out to the island's edge, to the spot where she'd last seen her mother, tightening the leather straps and belt and working the buckles of the parachute pack as best she could as she ran. At the edge, she stopped for a last split-second adjustment, gathered her courage, and dove over the side.

With her hands together in front of her and her ankles together behind, Brieze made her body into a long, slim knife that sliced through the air. The side of the island, all naked stone, porous and pitted, rushed up past her. Her long braid of jet-black hair whipped out straight behind her. She squinted as the wind stung and watered her eyes. There had been no time for goggles.

There was her mother! A few hundred yards below and to the left—a small human figure standing out against the silvery-gray sea of clouds below, clouds that would soon swallow her up. Brieze was glad to see her mother had kept her head. She wasn't flailing or screaming. She was doing what everyone had been instructed to do, from an early age, if you found yourself in free fall without a parachute. She was on her back, her arms and legs spread wide, presenting as much resistance to the wind as possible. The dress she wore, which Brieze had always considered ridiculous—the kind of baggy, impractical thing that could only be fashionable in a backwater village—was working to her advantage now. It was catching the wind and slowing her fall.

"*Mother!*" Brieze shouted. The wind tore the words from her mouth and spirited them away.

But Patentia heard her, or at least spotted her. She waved her arms to attract Brieze's attention. Brieze came out of her dive. She spread her arms wide and used the wings of her flightsuit to steer. She aimed straight for her mother's chest. She was close enough now to see the widened whites of her eyes, the flush on her cheeks. Patentia managed to look frightened, embarrassed, and angry all at the same time.

"Grab on! Don't let go!" Brieze shouted.

They smacked into each other.

The impact knocked the breath out of them, sent them spinning and tumbling. Brieze wrapped her arms and legs tightly around her mother. Her mother's limbs clamped around her. For seconds that seemed like forever, they gripped each other as hard as they could. There was no up, no down. Only each other. They became one body with eight limbs, two hearts thumping wildly against each other, and one mind begging the universe to let it live.

Soon, they stopped spinning. Their breath came back to them. Their grip on each other relaxed by a fraction of a squeeze. Brieze could tell up from down. She wrestled an arm free from her mother and pulled the ripcord of her parachute pack. The chute and its lines slithered out of the pack, and the chute expanded with a whump as it filled with air. They felt as if they were being yanked upward as the chute strained to slow their fall. Brieze looked down. The surface clouds were so close it seemed as if her dangling feet could touch them. Another few moments of free fall, and they would have fallen through those clouds and hit the very solid, very hard ground beneath them.

Brieze looked up. The floating island was far above them, looking like a jagged-edged rock suspended in the sky. Much too high to reach.

Brieze looked over at Selemont, the nearest mountain. It was close, and their best bet. Their only bet. At the very least, she thought, she should be able to land them safely in some field or orchard on its lower flanks. And she might get lucky and catch a mountain updraft that would carry them high enough to get back to the island again.

Patentia's chin nestled snugly into the crook of Brieze's neck and shoulder. Brieze asked if she was all right, and felt her nod in response. "I have to let go to steer," Brieze said. "Hold on."

Brieze reached for the steering toggles that dangled near her hands. Patentia held on. Though, as Brieze tugged on the toggle cords and steered them toward the mountain, she became aware that her mother wasn't gripping her with both hands. One set of her mother's fingers dug into her back, but the fingers of her other hand were closed into a fist that pressed against her, as if her mother were clutching something she didn't want to let go of.

They got lucky. The heavy winds hitting the sun-warmed mountain produced a strong updraft. As soon as Brieze steered close enough to see rows of golden ripe wheat and harvest-ready corn rippling with the gusts, close enough that she could have hailed the fieldworkers if she'd wanted to, the updraft caught and lifted them. They rose past the fields and orchards. Past the walled city of Selemont and the bustling traffic in its stone-paved streets. They rose right past the western wall of Castle Selestria. Soldiers manning the wall stared in surprise at the two women clinging to each other in midair, riding the precarious lift of a single parachute. But before the soldiers could call out and ask if they needed any help, Brieze and her mother were far above the castle.

Brieze looked down at the floating island. They would make it now. She relaxed. The knots in her stomach and her shoulders, which she hadn't even been aware of until now, loosened. She let out a relieved breath. So did her mother. But the next moment Patentia sucked in her breath again and let loose with a flurry of scolding words. Her mouth was right next to Brieze's ear, and she felt the heat of the words against her cheek. "Never, ever, *ever* in all your life do anything like that again! What were you thinking diving off the edge of the island like that? You had me scared to death. You could have been killed."

"Me!?" Brieze countered. "What about *you,* mother? What in the world were you doing standing near the edge of the island in that wind, muttering and talking to yourself like a crazy person?"

Patentia was quiet for a moment. "Tobias proposed to me," she finally said, as if this were a perfectly logical and reasonable answer.

Brieze let this sink in. It was strange to think of her mother with a man. It had always been just the two of them. Back in the small village on the tiny mountain known as Footmont where she grew up, no man ever considered marrying her mother, a woman with an illegitimate, out-of-wedlock child. But Brieze supposed she should have known this might change when she became the wizard's apprentice and they moved to his island. Her mother wasn't that old, thirty-five, and she was still good-looking, Brieze supposed, in a rustic, plumpish sort of way.

"Let's not have this conversation in midair," Brieze said.

Patentia nodded in agreement.

Brieze skimmed over the island at treetop level, looking for a place to land. On its flat topside, the island's surface was covered with grasses and mosses, scrub brush and hardy dwarf pines. Small ponds sparkled in the sunlight here and there, their surfaces rippling in the wind. Brieze floated right over the roof of the wizard's large, rambling house, with its towers and balconies, its cornices and cupolas. She waved to the people gathered out front. They waved back and cheered when they saw that Patentia was safe.

But Brieze didn't want to land near the house. She wanted somewhere more private, where they could talk. She chose a grassy field out of sight of the house. With the extra weight hanging on the chute, they had to come in low and fast.

"Rolling landing," Brieze said.

Her mother nodded. Every sky rider has an instinct for riding the wind, for soaring and swooping, even Patentia, who by sky rider standards was short and thickly built and clumsy. Brieze hit the field in the exact center. Her toes touched the ground, her mother's heels touched the ground, and they executed a rolling landing together, arms wrapped around each other. Patentia did a decent job, especially considering she faced backward as they touched down.

Lying on their sides in the grass, they disentangled themselves from the chute and from each other. They lay there for a few moments, just breathing, looking up at the sky and feeling the comforting solidness of the island beneath them. Brieze sat up and brushed the grass from her flightsuit. She pulled her long braid in front of her and ran her hands along it, cleaning it off. Stroking her braid this way always calmed her. "So," she said, "Tobias proposed. That's why you two are acting strange. I take it you didn't say yes?"

Patentia sat up and brushed herself off. She did this one-handed, still clutching something in a fist in her lap. "I told him I need to think about it."

"Are you in love with him?"

Patentia chewed her lower lip the way she did when thinking something over. Brieze recognized the gesture as one of her own. She understood her mother was debating what—or how much—to tell her. "It's complicated," Patentia finally said curtly, giving Brieze what she had always thought of as her mother's "hard face." It was a stern mask she used to hide her emotions. Brieze had seen the hard face nearly every day growing up on Footmont. But she rarely saw it since they joined the wizard's island community. Here, her mother had made real friends. She smiled a lot, and flirted with Tobias, and laughed—a genuine laugh, not the false cheer she used to employ.

With her "hard face" firmly set, Patentia tried to gather up her hair and tie it in a knot. But she was having trouble because of the thing she held in her hand.

"For heaven's sake, mother! What are you holding onto there like it's your last silver coin?"

Patentia let her hair go. She looked down at her clenched fist. She opened the fist and handed the object concealed there to Brieze. Her face softened. She handed the thing over as if it were the explanation she couldn't bring herself to put into words. All she said was, "I was trying to throw this over the side of the island. That's why I was standing so close to the edge. But I couldn't do it."

Brieze took the thing and studied it. It was a gray heart-shaped stone, worn smooth by some mountain stream and polished by years of constant handling. She had vague recollections of seeing the stone around their hut as a child. On one side, someone had carved the initials P and K. The other side of the stone was inscribed with the complicated characters used in the far-away Eastern Kingdoms. Brieze had been studying the Eastern language. It took her a moment to puzzle the characters out. They said, *may our love last forever.*

A jolt of anger stiffened her. She made a fist around the stone. "I remember this. It's from my father," she said. "Something he gave you."

Patentia nodded. "He found it on the bank of a stream, and he inscribed it. See how the P and the K are joined?"

Brieze didn't open her fist to look. She knew little about her biological father, and she didn't care to know more. She and her mother didn't talk about him anymore. His name was Kaishou Fujiwara, and he was a merchantman from the city of Kyo in the Eastern Kingdoms. At least that's what he'd told her mother. His ship, the *Atagu Maru*, had stopped at Footmont for a week for repairs and to take on water and provisions for the journey home. During that time, Kaishou and her mother had "fallen in love," as her mother put it.

Kaishou had promised to return and marry her mother, once he'd gotten his merchant vessel safely home and secured the permission of his family.

But Patentia never saw or heard from him again. She'd written him many letters, sent by way of trading ships to Kyo, but never got one back.

When Brieze thought about her father, which wasn't often, it opened a well of anger and sadness—and strangely, shame—in her. A well she preferred to keep tightly covered. As far as she was concerned, everything the man had said was a lie. She doubted Kaishou was even his real name. He'd seduced her mother, then disappeared. It was a story you heard often enough. When Brieze imagined her father, she pictured him drinking in some tavern, bragging to his friends about all the dumb farmers' and herders' daughters he'd bedded.

"So *this* is all he gave you," Brieze said with a sneer. "The rich merchant from Kyo. A *rock* with your initials scratched into it?"

"He wasn't rich. He was just a boy. And he was sweet. And kind." Patentia reached out and tucked a few loose strands of Brieze's straight, raven-black hair behind her ears, stroked the honey-colored skin of her cheek, looked wistfully into her daughter's black, almond-shaped eyes. "And anyway, the stone wasn't the *only* thing he gave me."

Brieze flushed, understanding her mother meant *her*. This made her even sadder and angrier. She looked nothing like her mother, who had reddish-brown curly hair, blue eyes, a smattering of freckles across her fair skin. Brieze looked like an Easterner, not a Westerner, and she had always hated her features—her straight black hair, the color of her skin, the shape of her eyes. All her life, they had marked her as different.

"You can't still be in love with him? After seventeen years?"

Patentia shrugged helplessly, looking down into her lap.

Brieze leapt to her feet. "That's ridiculous. If *you* can't throw this stupid stone away, mother, *I'll* do it for you." With that she stalked off, toward where she calculated the nearest edge of the island would be. Patentia got to her feet with a strangled sound and chased after her daughter. She tackled Brieze from behind, wrapping her arms around her waist and bringing them both to the ground with a thud. It was hard to say who was more surprised by this, daughter or mother. Brieze dropped the stone, and they wrestled for it, scrabbling and grunting. Patentia got it. She sat up and clutched the stone to her chest with both hands.

Then she doubled over, sobbing.

"He's out there somewhere…I feel it in my bones…he still loves me…one day he'll come back…"

Brieze blinked, stunned. Her anger evaporated. She may have noticed a lilt in her mother's voice, a gleam in her eye, whenever they'd talked about her father, but she never imagined her mother felt anything like this. And it was hard to believe that her mother, who had always been so tough and practical-minded, if not exactly smart, believed something so pathetically delusional. How had it happened? It must have been a story she told herself over and over, Brieze supposed, an illusion she clung to that helped her get through the toughest times, until she started to actually believe it.

Brieze chewed her lower lip. How could she help her mother? How could she free her of this delusion that kept her stuck in the past, that kept her from marrying a good man like Tobias and being happy? To her logical mind, there was only one answer. Gently, she gathered up her mother's flying hair and tied it into a windproof knot. She put her arms around her and held her until the sobbing fit subsided into sniffles. She found a handkerchief and offered it to Patentia, who used it to dab her eyes and blow her nose.

"Here's what we're going to do," Brieze said. "I'm going to find this man. This Kaishou Fujiwara from the city of Kyo. And I'm going to bring him here, willing or unwilling. He's going to look you in the eye and explain himself. He's going to tell you what he's been up to the past seventeen years, and whether he loves you or not. And then you can get on with your life."

TWO

The *Cygnet* was a small, creaky old ship, Tak noted with disappointment as he and his platoon of cadets climbed aboard. It was crewed by equally creaky old airmen, those too old for more dangerous duties and who needed easier work as they coasted toward retirement. The ship had been stripped down of everything not necessary to train cadets. The sails and rigging had been simplified. Six light cannon sat at regularly spaced intervals along either edge of the deck, their barrels pointing out at the sky, but all their gear, powder, and shot were stored securely below. They were tied up tight, and each fitted with a sign that said, *DON'T EVEN THINK ABOUT TOUCHING THIS.*

Tak sighed and pulled at the stiff collar of his cadet uniform. The gray wool uniform was a little too small for his tall, lanky frame. It felt tight and constricting around the shoulders, and the cuffs of its sleeves didn't quite reach his wrists. Also, it itched. Being a cadet at the academy was a lot less exciting than he'd imagined. In fact, so far, it had consisted of little more than following a bunch of strict and pointless rules. He and his fellow cadets had to be up at the crack of dawn, fully dressed and with their beds neatly made. They had to arrive at the mess hall precisely at six a.m. for breakfast and be finished by six-thirty. Every hour of the day after that was scheduled for them—an endless series of lectures and drills and physical training.

Failure to follow any of the rules or to be where you were supposed to be at the precise time you were supposed to be there resulted in demerits, which resulted in punishments. The punishments mostly involved scrubbing. Scrubbing pots in the mess hall kitchen—or worse—scrubbing the latrines. Tak, who had recently turned sixteen, was not a rule follower by nature. Already, he'd done his share of scrubbing. He hadn't realized how free and easy his life had been before.

"Don't even *look* at those cannons!" the drill sergeant growled, noticing some of the cadets gazing longingly at them. "We'll not be taking cannon practice today. We'll be seeing how you keep your feet on an airship while swinging a sword."

Some of the cadets' hands went to the hilts of the swords strapped to their belts, as if to make sure they were still there. Tak tried to stick his hands in his pockets—but discovered for the umpteenth time that his cadet's breeches had no pockets. He ran a hand through his short-cropped, bristly brown hair, which had once been long and shaggy. He felt his sword hanging like a dead weight from his hip. He knew they would get to sword practice eventually, and he'd been dreading it. He hadn't swung his sword since the siege of Selestria, and the idea of wielding it filled him with an inexplicable fear.

The sergeant ordered Tak's platoon to stand at ease in the bow, out of the crew's way as the *Cygnet* was launched.

Like most airships of Etherium, the *Cygnet* looked something like an old-fashioned wooden sailing ship. But it was much wider and shallower in the hull, and the long keel dipped much deeper below it, the better to keep the ship upright and stable in the thick atmosphere. The *Cygnet* was tied snugly in its berth at the academy dock, built near the summit of Larkspur, a spur of Selemont that was home to the airfleet academy. With the sail furled, the ship hung heavily on its mooring lines, stretching them taut. But when the crew unfurled the sail and raised it up between the tall mainmast and slightly shorter foremast, the ship began to rise. The huge triangular sail filled with wind. It stretched on a long, flexible yard well over both sides of the ship, looking like a giant wing.

The *Cygnet* tried to rise on the wind, straining and tugging at the mooring lines that held it down. The wooden deck under Tak's feet came alive, thrumming and pitching. He smiled. He couldn't help but be reminded of his own little craft, the *Arrow*, and how with a raised sail it always seemed eager to slip its mooring lines and soar into the sky.

"Launch!" the captain called from the command deck.

"Brace yourselves," the sergeant ordered.

The crew tugged on knots and released all four mooring lines simultaneously, and with a whoosh the *Cygnet* took flight. Tak felt the thrill in the pit of his stomach as he was momentarily weightless and the ship skimmed out into the sky. The wind ruffled his hair. The cadets grinned. The old crewmen grinned. Even the dour drill sergeant had something like a grin on his face. This was the soaring feeling of freedom every sky rider craved. The cadets kept their feet as the ship listed one way, then the other, finding its balance. The crew adjusted the angle and position of the sail. They unfurled a stabilizing sail from the bowsprit.

The crew had orders to cruise the sky around Larkspur, keeping the *Cygnet* steady but throwing in the occasional surprise lurch or roll. Some crewmen hauled up practice dummies from below deck and placed them in the spaces between each cannon. The dummies were just wooden poles with straw-filled sacks tied around them and much-battered old helmets nailed to their tops. Each cadet took his place before one of the dummies, back straight, hand near the hilt of his sword.

"Present arms!" the drill sergeant shouted.

The cadets drew their swords and held them upright for inspection. Tak's sword parted reluctantly from its sheath. The weapon felt heavy and clumsy in his hand, not at all like an extension of his arm as it should have felt. It trembled slightly as he held it up, and Tak silently cursed his shaking hand.

The drill sergeant walked down the line of cadets, inspecting each weapon. Some were family weapons, given to the boys by their fathers as Tak's had been. Others were issued by the academy. Regardless, the fledgling cadets were expected to keep the weapons in tiptop shape. The sergeant grunted approvingly as he moved down the line of boys, eyes running expertly up and down each razor-sharp and freshly gleaming blade.

That is, until he got to Tak.

"What's this?" the sergeant frowned.

Tak's sword gleamed as brightly as any of the others. But the edges of the blade were nicked and dull. Tak flushed. Still, he stood with his back straight and eyes forward, as cadets were supposed to do.

The sergeant was disappointed. He'd been eager to see what the boy could do. Taktinius Spinner junior was famous for fighting in the siege of Selestria—among other things. The King himself had presented Tak with a medal of valor and ordered his acceptance into the academy. The sergeant had hoped the boy would give a performance of swordsmanship that would inspire the other cadets.

"This weapon is a disgrace," the sergeant said. "That blade's not fit to cut butter. What have you been doing with it, hacking at mill stones?"

"No sir," Tak replied. "Gublin armor."

The sergeant's eyebrows shot up. The cadets didn't dare whisper among each other, but they exchanged glances. "So!" the sergeant said. "You think because you fought in one short battle you've got the right to show up with an unfit weapon and give me back talk?"

"No sir," Tak said. "I meant no disrespect."

"And you mean to tell me you haven't sharpened your blade since the siege? What kind of soldier are you?"

Several replies occurred to Tak, but he wisely kept his mouth shut.

"Well," the sergeant took a step backward, put his hands on his hips, and raised his voice to make sure every cadet and crewman heard. "Our young hero has earned himself another demerit. And cleanup detail after mess tonight."

A few snorts of laughter, quickly stifled, escaped from the cadets. The drill sergeant ignored them. Some of Tak's fellows at the academy were in awe of him, but just as many, if not more, were jealous. There were even rumors going around that Tak hadn't fought in the siege at all. That the story was made up.

The sergeant raised his voice another notch. "And if our hero doesn't want a second night of cleanup duty, he will demonstrate an expert two-handed crosscut blow followed by an overhead blow that knocks the helmet clear off this dummy. Think you can handle that, boy?"

Tak nodded.

The sergeant took a few more steps back, giving Tak space to swing his sword. "Then get to it. Show us how you killed those Gublins."

Tak stepped up to the dummy, gripping his sword with both hands. His palms were sweaty. His mouth had gone dry. He was keenly aware that every pair of eyes was on him. Silence fell over the *Cygnet*. The old ship's wooden beams groaned. Ropes creaked. From somewhere in the rigging above, a crewman coughed. The practice dummy loomed over Tak. It had grown taller, somehow. The empty eye slits of its rusty, dented helmet glared at him menacingly.

Show us how you killed those Gublins.

Tak swung—and in that instant he was no longer on the deck of the *Cygnet*.

He was on the walls of Castle Selestria, trying not to die.

Men were screaming.

The city was on fire.

His fighting partner, the huge lumberjack Jon Cutter, collapsed in a heap, the life leaking out of him from a gash in his neck.

Instead of a dummy looming over Tak, there was an armored Gublin soldier with a curved sword in each hand. He easily parried Tak's blow and struck back blindingly fast—as if with four or five swords at once. Tak's shield shattered. His sword was knocked out of his hands. A blade stabbed into the center of his chest. Tak screamed and toppled backward.

At least, that's what happened in Tak's head.

On the *Cygnet*, everyone saw Tak give the dummy a clumsy blow, lose his grip on his sword, fall to the deck with a scream and curl up into a quivering ball.

After a moment of shocked silence, they all crowded around him and began jostling and talking at once. "Stand back! *Back*, everyone!" the drill sergeant ordered, shoving curious cadets aside. He knelt next to Tak and put a hand on his shoulder. The boy was shaking like a sail torn loose in a storm. The sergeant sometimes doubted whether the boy really had fought on the castle walls during the siege. He wondered if Tak hadn't at least exaggerated his role in the battle. But the sergeant doubted no longer. He was an experienced soldier, and he'd seen the mental aftereffects of combat, especially in young men after their first real fight.

To the inexperienced cadets, however, Tak's actions seemed to prove just the opposite.

"*This* is our hero who won the medal of valor?" one snorted.

"He never fought in no battle," another muttered.

"They should send him back to the spider farms, let him weave sails like the rest of his family," a third joined in.

✳ ✳ ✳

They ambushed Tak after dinner as he was finishing his cleanup duties. He pushed a wheelbarrow loaded with trash and plate scrapings up a muddy mountainside path through the woods toward a muddy clearing that was home to the academy's garbage pit. The pit had been dug far away from the academy buildings. Tak grunted and cursed as he struggled to push the heavy wheelbarrow up the rutted, stone-clogged path. He sweated itchily under his uniform. He was trying, unsuccessfully, to keep the mud off his boots. He'd have to clean and polish them for inspection tomorrow morning.

The sun sat low in the purple evening sky, dipping toward dusk, its rays slanting through the trunks of the trees. Hairs prickled on the back of Tak's neck. Someone was watching him. He dropped the wheelbarrow handles and whipped around. There was no one on the path behind him. He turned in a full circle, scanning the woods on both sides and the path ahead. All empty. Of course, there could be a platoon of cadets in the woods around him, hiding behind the trunks of trees, and he'd never see them. Frowning, he picked up the handles and resumed his struggle with the wheelbarrow.

The garbage pit had been widened each year until it took up the entire clearing. The academy had in fact hired loggers to cut down trees and make more space. Tak had seen some of them eating in the mess hall, at a table in the back by the kitchen. Rough-looking men with bushy beards and bulging arms. He knew they had a camp somewhere out in these woods. Freshly cut stumps ringed the clearing, and several felled trees lay on the ground, in the process of being sawed into lumber. Tak's ambushers let him dump his load of garbage into the pit, wipe his sweaty brow, and turn around, making ready to head down the path back to the mess hall, before they emerged from the woods.

There were three of them. Older boys. All with the short-cropped hair and gray uniforms of cadets. Tak recognized their faces, but couldn't recall their names. With hundreds of cadets at the academy, there hadn't been time to learn all the names yet. He especially recognized the leader of the group, the biggest boy who emerged from the woods first. Tak had heard his brash voice raised in the mess hall and seen the way he shouldered ahead of the younger cadets in the chow line. The other two ambushers stood on either side of him, smiling wickedly.

Tak shoved the wheelbarrow aside and faced the leader, who had a few inches, not to mention several pounds, on him. The bully looked down at Tak with mock disgust. "I thought we'd find this piece of garbage out here," he said.

His buddies snickered.

Tak flushed and his hands instinctively balled into fists. But he made himself breathe slowly and calmly. He unclenched his hands. Fighting was strictly forbidden among cadets. It was cause for immediate dismissal from the academy. Even so, from what Tak gathered during mess hall conversations, it happened all the time. He was sure there was going to be a fight. That's why the boys chose this isolated ambush spot. But he wasn't going to be the one to throw the first punch. That way, at least he could claim he'd been defending himself.

"That's very clever," Tak said. "You're a funny guy. What do you want?"

"*What do you want?*" the boy snorted and mocked Tak's tone. "I heard you were real impressive at sword practice this morning. Put on quite a show."

Tak flushed again. His failure that morning had been mortifying. They'd taken him to the infirmary and let him rest for a few hours. When he'd recovered, they'd let him go back to his lessons and drills. He'd fixed his gaze on his boots for the rest of the day, embarrassed to look anyone in the eye, to see the disappointment and pity that was sure to be there. At dinner, some of the guys in his platoon, all decent boys who he considered friends, sat with him to show their support. But no one knew what to say. They'd eaten in awkward silence. He had been grateful for his cleanup duties which allowed him to escape the mess hall and help the kitchen staff wash dishes.

"You wouldn't understand," Tak said.

"*You wouldn't understand,*" the boy echoed. "Well, I understand this. You're a coward. And a liar. You never fought in the siege of Selestria. You don't deserve a place at this academy. So we're gonna teach you a lesson."

There was a time, not long ago, when being called a coward and a liar would have had Tak instantly swinging his fists. Just a few months ago, but seemingly forever ago, he'd overheard Admiral Scud call him a liar while he was spying on a meeting between the admiral and the wizard. The accusation had been enough to make him blow his cover and confront the admiral. Things had not gone particularly well after that.

This time Tak kept his cool. He'd grown up a bit since then. *He* knew what the truth was, and that was all that mattered. What other people thought mattered less to him. "Speaking of cowards," he said. "What do you call a guy who needs three-to-one odds to teach me a lesson?"

That barb hit home. The boy's face twisted into an ugly snarl. He would have attacked right then had not all of them been startled by a loud *crack*! behind them. It was the sound of a large branch being broken off a tree. They all turned to see where the sound came from. A boy stepped out of the woods near the path that led back down to the mess hall. He carried the large branch casually over his shoulder.

Boy was not the first word Tak would have used to describe the newcomer. *Scrawny giant* was the phrase that came to mind. He couldn't be much older than Tak, but he was already close to seven feet tall. His frame was huge, all wide

shoulders and long limbs, but it looked as if he'd been growing so fast there'd been no time to put any meat on his
bones. His arms were thin and wiry, with knobby wrists and
elbows, and the knotty tree branch seemed like an extension
of them. He wasn't a cadet. He wore workman's clothes.
Something about the boy was familiar to Tak, especially his
curly, fiery red hair and his scruffy, patchy red beard.

"Them odds just got better," the boy said in a deep, gruff
voice.

The lead bully sputtered for a moment in confusion.
"Who the hell are *you*?" he asked.

The scrawny giant didn't answer. Instead, he chewed the
beard under his lower lip, cleared his throat with a growl,
and spit at their feet. With that, Tak realized why the boy
seemed familiar. Tak's fighting partner during the siege of
Selestria, the tree-sized Jon Cutter, had chewed his red
beard and spit over the castle ramparts in just the same way
before the battle. This boy must be one of the Cutters, a family of loggers who lived on Pinemont. He must be part of the
group hired to clear the trees.

The bullies seemed to recognize the boy as a Cutter as
well, judging from how they hesitated. The Cutters of Pinemont were well known throughout the Kingdom of Spire for
their size and toughness, their ability to fell prodigious
amounts of trees with huge axes, and for their bad tempers
when crossed.

The bullies' leader shook off his hesitation. "You two
take the tall freak," he directed his cronies. "I'll handle our
hero here."

They leapt into action.

Things happened fast.

A loud *whack*! sounded in the clearing. The scrawny giant had swung his long arms, and his long branch connected with the skull of one of his attackers, evening the odds to two-on-two before any of the boys had gotten close enough to trade punches.

The charging leader closed on Tak and swung. Tak had little formal training in hand-to-hand combat so far, but he had good instincts and he was fast. He sidestepped and shoved, tripping up his attacker's legs. The boy's fist missed and he went down in the mud, falling to his hands and knees. Unfortunately, Tak lost his footing on the slippery ground and went down too, sprawling on his back. The boy was on top of him in an instant. As they rolled and grappled in the mud, each trying to get on top and pin the other, Tak heard another *whack*! of wood against skull somewhere close by.

The lead bully was bigger than Tak, stronger, and had the benefit of more training. He straddled Tak's chest, pinning his arms with his legs. Tak writhed and cursed and kicked but couldn't shake the boy off. The boy raised a fist to drive into Tak's face. "This…" he said, gasping for breath, "is what happens to liars." Tak shut his eyes and made a strangled sound.

The blow never landed.

There was a third and final *whack*!

The boy's eyes rolled up into his head and he toppled sideways off of Tak.

The Cutter boy stood looming over him, leaning on his tree branch like a staff. He held out a hand and helped Tak up. He was an odd-looking one. It seemed that the features of his face had decided to stop growing in a coordinated fashion and instead race each other pell-mell to adulthood. His ears were in the lead. But his nose wasn't far behind. He was too young to grow a full beard but apparently determined to do so anyway, judging by the thin, patchy, aspiring beard that was doing its best to cover his face. On his feet, Tak tried to wipe the mud off his uniform and out of his hair, which only coated his hands with mud, which he wiped onto his breeches.

"Who are you?" he asked.

As he would learn later, the Cutter boy had a habit of not answering questions. He was also a man of few words, most of the time. He took a piece of folded-up paper from a pocket and handed it to Tak. "You write this?" he asked.

Tak unfolded the paper. It was smudged with grime and old blood.

John Cutter, Pinemont was written there. Tak's sergeant during the siege of Selestria had written that. This was the paper they pinned to Jon Cutter to identify him before his body had been shipped home. Below the name, in Tak's hand, was written, *He was a brave man. He loved you all. I am sorry. Tak Spinner.*

Tak nodded and handed the paper back.

The boy grunted and looked Tak up and down, as if taking a mental picture of him. "Thanks," he said. "It helped."

"You're welcome," Tak said. "I'm glad. He was a good

man."

"Did he really say that, before he died? That he loved us?"

"He did."

The boy's Adam's apple bobbed up and down. His ears turned red. He gritted his teeth. "I shoulda been there," he said. "I coulda done something maybe."

Tak shook his head. He put a hand on the boy's shoulder. "Believe me, there was nothing you could have done."

The boy's fingers squeezed his tree branch, hard. "They wouldn't let me go. I shoulda gone anyway."

"If you did, you'd probably be dead too. And anyway, you're too young to fight."

"*You're* too young, but you were there."

"That was a mistake. Some bad luck."

The boy took a deep breath. His ears faded back to their usual color. He held out his hand. "Jon Cutter junior, of Pinemont."

Tak shook his hand. "Taktinius Spinner junior, Selemont. I'm sorry about your dad."

The boy shrugged and looked down at his boots, out of words.

"Are you with the loggers?" Tak asked, to fill the silence.

It took a while for the Cutter boy to answer. "Yep. Followed you from the mess hall. Just wanted to say thanks. Gonna head to camp now." He nodded a brief farewell and stalked off toward the woods. Tak was too surprised by the encounter to think of anything else to say. The boy said over his shoulder, "Might want to get outta here before those three come around."

The three cadets on the ground were beginning to groan and stir.

"One more thing," the Cutter boy said, turning around and looking Tak in the eye. "You need anything, just holler. Okay?"

"Okay," Tak said.

The scrawny giant disappeared into the woods.

THREE

"Wait until the spring, until after the Wizard's Summit," the wizard urged. "Then I can go with you. I've been meaning to make a trip to the Eastern Kingdoms."

Brieze shook her head. She wanted to go alone. And she didn't want to wait until spring. The sooner she found and returned with Kaishou Fujiwara, and got the whole unpleasant business finished, the sooner her mother could get on with her life. If she left soon, she could complete the two-and-a-half month voyage before winter set in and the harsh temperatures and heavy winds made the trip more difficult and dangerous. Her plan was to spend the winter in the city of Kyo, searching for the man, and return with him in the spring.

The wizard had invited her out for a walk. They strolled along one of the paths that meandered around the island. The sky was a cheery morning green, the wind brisk. Dry leaves rustled on the trees and clouds chased each other overhead. They wore cloaks against the fall chill. Brieze knew the wizard would use the walk to try to talk her out of going. He never did anything without some larger purpose or intention behind it.

"I've tried to teach you patience," he sighed, "but it's not something that comes naturally to one of your age." He took a parental tone with her because he was, in fact, her father. Legally anyway. Wizards don't marry. They designate their apprentices as legal heirs. But since Brieze didn't have a father, the wizard had gone a step further and formally adopted her, too.

Though he said the words in a kindly way, she bristled at the criticism.

"You think I shouldn't go alone?" she asked. "Do you think I can't take care of myself?"

The wizard frowned, deepening the wrinkles around his mouth. His usually serene blue eyes looked troubled beneath their white brows. "I know you can more than handle yourself," he said. "You proved that when I sent you to talk to the Gublins. It's just that...those wolves that attacked you..."

"That wasn't your fault," she said. "You don't have to keep apologizing."

"But it *was* my fault. I never would have sent you if I'd known wolves had established themselves beneath the surface clouds. I didn't think it was possible. My ignorance, my miscalculation, put you at risk." The wizard halted, forcing Brieze to stop too. He faced her and took her hands in his. "There will be many dangers on this trip. I can give you protections against the ones I know. But it's the dangers I don't know about that worry me." He sighed and offered her a sad smile. "Worrying. It's a parent's prerogative you know."

Brieze dropped her eyes and chewed at the corner of her lower lip. A pang of guilt squirmed in her belly. For a moment, she doubted her decision. She would be gone a long time, and there would be danger. She would make the people she cared about worry. Not only the wizard but her mother. And Tak. Did she have the right to do that?

The wizard, as usual, seemed to know what she was thinking. He was not the type of person to manipulate anyone with guilt. "Nevertheless, you must follow your conscience my dear, and trust your instincts. If you spend your life trying to take care of other people's feelings, you'll find you have time for little else."

Brieze smiled at him gratefully. "Thank you, father."

He gave her hands a squeeze. They resumed walking. The wizard turned them down a path to their right. "Of course, you'll need a sturdy ship for such a journey," he said.

"I've been working on that," she said. "I have a little money saved up. And I saw some ships at the auction lot in Selestria that would do."

"You could try that," the wizard said. "Or…" and here a certain lilt crept into his voice, and his eyes sparkled. "I might have something on the island that could serve."

Brieze caught that lilt in her father's voice. They had reached a little corner of the island that served as its tiny airfield. Just a clearing of bare ground surrounded by a few low -built wooden hangars and sheds where the wizard's shipwright and his assistants repaired and maintained the island's small collection of airships. The place was deserted.

The wizard never did anything without some larger purpose or intention behind it.

He led Brieze to one of the wooden hangars. Her stomach did an excited flip as he grasped the handle of the sliding
door. "This is a prototype ship I've been working on with
our shipwright. A voyage to the Eastern Kingdoms would
make a good test run. I should warn you it's not quite ready
yet, but with a little extra work it could be ready soon." A
sly grin spread across his face.

An answering, wondering, not-daring-to-hope-but-hoping
-anyway grin spread across her face.

The wizard slid the door open…

✳ ✳ ✳

"Hot dragon's balls!" Tak exclaimed. "I've never *seen* a
ship like this." He was grinning, exuberant. He'd escaped
the academy with a weekend pass and come to visit Brieze
on the island. He'd ditched his cadet uniform and was back
in his old, comfortable clothes. She had, of course, taken
him straight to the airfield to see her new ship. They'd
agreed to take it out for its first flight together.

The ship wasn't unusual in design or construction. The
lines of its hull and the curves of its wings were similar to
Tak's *Arrow*, though less streamlined. What was completely,
mind-boggling different about the ship was its color. Or to
be precise, its *lack* of color. Inside the dark hangar, the ship
had looked black. But when they dragged it out onto the
bare ground of the airfield, it turned an earth-toned tan.

When they dragged it a little farther to a patch of grassy ground near the island's edge, the ship turned a grassy green. The hull, the masts, even the sail and rudder changed color. The only parts of the ship that stayed their natural hue were the ropes and rigging, the brass hardware, and the wooden deck, which was hidden below the gunwales.

"It's a new pigment my father developed," Brieze explained. "It assumes the predominant color in its environment. It should make for effective camouflage."

"You'll be invisible in the sky," Tak said with a marveling grin. "How devious! You could sneak up on anybody."

"Or sneak *past* anybody." Brieze smiled. She liked that word, *devious*.

They strained and sweated as they used ropes to drag the ship to the launch ramp at the island's edge. Small airships are built to be as light as possible. Two people can usually drag one easily. But Brieze's ship was heaver. It was built for stability and endurance, not speed. When they reached the lip of the launch ramp, they rested, catching their breath.

Brieze gazed eagerly at the sky, using a nearby flock of birds to read the currents. Like every sky rider, she craved the weightless freedom of flying. The anticipation of it gave her a fluttery feeling in her belly. Her pulse quickened. Tak felt it too. And for sky riders there was nothing like taking a virgin ship out for its maiden voyage, watching it respond to the wind's embrace, feeling it rise and soar and stretch its wings. Tak watched Brieze as she watched the sky. Loose strands of her silky black hair fluttered around her face. Her cheeks were pink with the wind. Her lips were parted. Her black eyes glistened.

"What?" she said, realizing he was staring at her.

"You're beautiful," Tak answered.

Brieze started to smile, then caught herself and quirked her mouth into a less approving expression. "Keep your mind on the sky, pirate," she said with as much sternness as she could muster. "And your amorous feelings to yourself."

"Aye aye, captain," Tak said. "For now."

Brieze bit down on her grin again.

They raised the sail, adjusted it to the proper angle, and made sure all the ropes and rigging were working correctly. The standard way to launch such a ship was to run it downhill off the slanting side of a mountain. On the flat-topped island, they had to use the ramp. They checked each other's parachute packs. They clipped their lifelines to the aft mast. They each took a position behind one of the short wings that sprouted from either side of the craft, gripping an edge. They nodded their readiness to each other, then ran down the ramp, pushing the airship ahead of them.

As the ship gained speed, the air rushing over and under the curved front edge of the sail gave it lift. When they felt it rise, they hopped in over the gunwales. The sail filled and strained with a loud flap and a *whuff*—and they were free of the island, airborne, rising fast on an updraft. Every brand-new rope on the ship creaked as if letting out a little squeal of delight.

They grinned at each other wildly, their faces flushed and sweaty. Before he knew what he was doing, Tak threw his arms around Brieze and gave her a long, deep, joyous kiss.

She kissed him back, her heart skipping beats. It was a perfect moment. The two of them weightless. The wind stirring their hair. They had kissed before, but never quite like this. For a moment, they wished they weren't on an airship at all, but someplace where they could kiss longer. A lot longer…

But an airship is no place for making out. Not if you want to get back to the ground in one piece. Reluctantly, they parted. Brieze took the tiller—it was her ship, after all—while Tak lowered the keel. It dropped into place with a satisfying wooden clunk, and the rocking ship stabilized. Tak's thumping heart settled down to a more orderly beat. They saw with delight that the ship had taken on the blue hue of the noon sky. But it was oddly disconcerting too. It made them feel as if the ship weren't quite real, that nothing was holding them up in the air. They were glad the deck under their feet remained its reliable, substantial woody color.

"Let's give this ship a shakedown," Tak said. "And see how you handle it."

When she told him of her plan to journey to the Eastern Kingdoms, Tak had insisted on taking leave from the academy to go with her. But she had refused him. For every argument he came up with for why he should join her, she countered only that she needed to make the trip alone. He finally relented with one condition—that he give her some flying lessons that would help her on her voyage. Unlike Tak, who began learning to fly on his father's knee as soon as he was old enough to grasp a tiller and a rope, Brieze hadn't done much flying when she was younger. On Footmont, there hadn't been many opportunities. She was a decent pilot, but she didn't have the instinct for flying that came from being raised with airships.

They headed north, keeping to the western side of the Highspire Mountains. Selemont stood immediately to starboard. Other mountains—Pinemont, Gatmont, Greenmont—stretched off into the northerly distance a few points off the starboard bow, losing themselves in the haze. A thunderstorm brewed above Pinemont. Anvil-like thunderheads congregated above its peak, with gray curtains of mist gathering beneath them. Tak stood in the bow while Brieze sat in the stern, working the tiller, ropes, and pedals. She used the mountain updrafts to climb to cruising altitude, angling the sail front downward for maximum lift.

"Let's practice turns first," Tak said. "Hard about to port."

Brieze used the pedal controls at her feet to put the left wing flap up, the right down. At the same time, she pushed the tiller hard to the right. The ship banked steeply and suddenly, making a lurching, wobbling left turn that nearly tumbled Tak off his feet. He grabbed onto a stay to steady himself. Brieze brought the wing flaps back to neutral position and pulled in the tiller. The ship steadied and straightened out.

"Whoa," Tak said. "That was a little rough."

"This tiller is too sensitive," Brieze huffed, her cheeks growing hot. "And the pedals feel stiff."

"New ships are like that. They take a little getting used to and wearing in. Let's practice some more turns."

They practiced port and starboard turns for half an hour.

Brieze got a better feel for the new ship, and her turns improved. But her earlier amorous feelings for Tak gave way to a creeping annoyance. She resented him, standing in the bow and barking orders at her like he was some kind of captain. She was used to giving orders, not taking them. She didn't like it when people knew more than her or were better than her at something. Especially when they were her boyfriend. And especially when they lorded it over her like Tak was doing. She tried to suppress the annoyance, telling herself it was petty.

In truth, Tak *was* lording it over her. He couldn't help himself. Sometimes, it was tough being Brieze's boyfriend. She wasn't just smarter than him, she was a *lot* smarter. She was better than him at nearly everything. Her marksmanship with a bow was better. She beat him at chess without even trying. One of the few things he could do better than her was pilot an airship. So he was enjoying himself. He tried to hide it and act nonchalant, but on the inside he was grinning and swaggering.

He wasn't hiding it nearly as well as he thought.

"Your turns are much better," he said. "Let's try hovering."

Brieze groaned. Hovering was one of the most complicated and difficult things to do with an airship. You had to pull on the rope that raised the front edge of the sail, creating wind resistance and slowing the ship almost to a stall. Then, just before it stalled out, you had to pull another rope, lowering the front edge of the sail and giving the ship speed and lift again. By alternately tugging on the two ropes, you were supposed to be able to keep the ship hovering, or at least bobbing, more or less in one spot. A seasoned flyer in a familiar ship could feel just by the tension in the ropes when to gently pull, when to slack, and keep her ship almost perfectly still. But Brieze struggled. She tugged one rope too hard, then overcompensated with the other. The ship jerked up and down, forward and backward. Tak gripped the foremast hard to steady himself.

"Not bad for your first time in a new ship," he said, offering her what he thought was an encouraging smile.

Brieze frowned and glowered at him. He was patronizing her! How *dare* he.

"Let's try something easier," he suggested. "Let's see you put this ship into a dive."

Diving was easier than hovering. All you had to do was lower both wing flaps and pull the front edge of the sail completely down. The bow would dip downward and the ship would drop with its own weight. A sly smile crept across Brieze's face. Her black eyes glittered with mischief. She wanted to wipe that condescending look off Tak's face, and she knew just how to do it. They were cruising above Sharpspur, a small rocky outcrop of Selemont. Sharpspur was not a habitable place, just a collection of giant, jagged stones poking knifelike out of the surface clouds.

Perfect, Brieze thought as she put the ship into a dive.

Objects fall slowly in the buoyant atmosphere of Etherium. A diving airship is no exception. Still, as the sail went slack and the prow split the air, they picked up enough speed to get the wind whipping past their faces and their adrenaline flowing. The ship pointed down at a forty-five degree angle, but it looked and felt to Brieze as if it were pointing *straight* down. She and Tak hooked their feet under straps on the deck and held on tight to stays.

"Okay," Tak said, his voice a little shaky. "Come out of it now."

Brieze's sly smile spread wider. The ship plunged faster. Every taut rope began to quiver and hum. The empty sail chattered. The jagged stones of Sharpspur rushed up from below.

"Now!" Tak's voice cracked with fear. "Now!"

That was enough to satisfy Brieze. She was just about to bring the ship out of its dive when something hit the side with a loud whump! The impact made the ship shudder.

Whump! Something else hit with an explosion of feathers.

Whump! Another one…

Birds! It was a flock of birds! They couldn't see the ship and were flying smack into it.

The birds only distracted Brieze for a few seconds. But a few seconds was enough to turn her reckless dive into something truly dangerous. Sharpspur was close now, *really* close. Close enough to see splotches of lichen on the jagged rocks. She raised the front edge of the sail and brought the flaps back to neutral. The ship levelled out, skimming through the sky with the speed it had gathered.

The keel below them hit one of the jagged tips of Sharpspur with a *crunch*!

The ship bounced like a stone skipping across water.

Crunch! The keel hit again and the ship bounced and lurched sideways, nearly capsizing. Brieze wrestled with the tiller, keeping the ship upright. Tak was thrown off his feet and came down on the deck hard.

Crunch! They hit one last time and then they were free of Sharpspur. The ship skated out into open sky. Brieze got it back under control.

Tak picked himself up off the deck. His face was pale. "You did that on purpose...why?"

Brieze was shaken, and the truth spilled out of her. "To wipe that damn smug look off your face."

Tak's eyes widened and his jaw dropped. Then his mouth snapped tightly shut. He shoved his hands into his pockets. He looked hurt and angry at the same time. Brieze hung her head. She felt awful. Like sick-to-her-stomach awful. She'd always suspected that, deep down, she was a lousy person. Now she knew it. She'd nearly killed them both, just to play a trick on him and gratify her ego. She concentrated on flying the ship back to the island. Tak sat in the bow. He didn't give her any orders.

It was a quiet trip.

A small wooden dock projected from the island's edge at a secluded spot not far from the wizard's house. As Brieze steered the ship toward the dock, Tak wordlessly got up and stood in the bow, holding a mooring line. Brieze executed a good docking maneuver, flying into the wind, angling the sail farther back the closer they approached, creating drag and slowing the ship to a crawl. The bow gently grazed the dock and Tak stepped off. He made the ship fast with the mooring line. He held a hand out to Brieze to help her out of the ship. But he avoided her eyes. She took his hand, and then they were standing awkwardly together on the dock.

That little dock happened to be where they first met. Brieze had confronted Tak and his friend Luff there as they were trying to sneak onto the island. Tak and Brieze had pointed arrows at each other and exchanged less-than-polite words. And Tak's friend Luff had executed a much-less-than-perfect docking maneuver, crashing into the dock and throwing Tak off the bow of the *Arrow* to land like a sack of turnips at Brieze's feet. The ghost of a smile flitted across Tak's face as he remembered. Being on the little dock softened his mood.

"I'm sorry," Brieze said in a small voice.

He put his arms around her. She circled hers gratefully around him. Their hearts were still thumping fast.

"I was being an ass," Tak said. "I'm sorry, too."

"I'll never do anything like that again. Promise."

Tak smiled. "It wasn't the first time you almost got me killed," he said with a sigh. "Probably won't be the last."

She punched him on the shoulder. "You do just fine almost getting yourself killed all on your own."

They hugged again, and neither said anything for a long time. They were realizing that soon Brieze would be gone, and it would be a long time before they saw each other again. Tak finally broke the silence. "This isn't like last time, is it? When you went to talk to the Gublins, and you wanted me to come along, but you wouldn't *say* you wanted me to come along?"

She lifted her head and looked into his shining brown eyes with a wistful smile. "No, this isn't like last time. I promise."

Part of her yearned for Tak to go with her. A big part. But then she imagined him being there when she confronted Kaishou Fujiwara. She was ashamed of her father, ashamed of the man she knew him to be. It would be an emotionally charged meeting. All those feelings she tried so hard to suppress might burst free. The anger, sadness, shame, and who knew what else? She didn't want anybody to see her like that. *Couldn't* let anybody see her like that. It would make her feel more exposed and vulnerable than being stripped naked.

That was the reason she needed to make the journey alone.

"If you're not back in the spring I'm coming to get you," he said.

"Deal," she said.

Something hit the dock with a clunk they felt in the soles of their feet. Brieze's ship, secured by only one mooring line, pitched and yawed about, listing and banging against the dock.

"Let's get a stern line on it," Tak said.

When they tied up the stern as well as the bow, the ship stabilized. It strained against the ropes, trying to rise, bobbing on the gusts of wind. The sky was shifting from noon blue to afternoon lavender, and the ship shifted color with it. It looked like a ship not made from wood and nails and rope, but molded from the same mysterious stuff the sky was made of.

Tak smiled at the way the sly little ship seemed so eager to take to the sky again. "Hey," he said. "What are you going to name it?"

The answer came to Brieze instantly. Her black eyes sparkled. "The *Devious*," she said. "I'll call it the *Devious*."

Tak grinned a rueful grin. He felt sorry for anyone in the Eastern Kingdoms who would be unlucky enough to run afoul of the *Devious* and her captain.

"Perfect," he said.

FOUR

Brieze chose the hour before sunrise as her departure time in the hope it would discourage people from showing up to see her off. She would be expected to make a farewell speech. It was traditional. She hated talking in front of people. So the fact that a small group of them had, in fact, gathered on the little dock in the predawn dimness, shivering in their cloaks, irritated her. Her mother was there of course. And the wizard. But there was also the wizard's cook, whom Brieze sometimes chatted with about recipes. And there were the goat herder twins Thomas and Timothy, who had an almost telepathic connection to their goats. There were a few women from the household—friends of her mother. And there was Tobias, standing awkwardly off by himself.

The next moment, Brieze was irked that *more* people hadn't shown up. The scanty attendance at her sendoff confirmed, in her mind, that people didn't like her. But she pushed her irritation aside. She couldn't have it both ways. And she couldn't blame people for not showing up. She knew she didn't have the knack for making friends. Growing up on Footmont, she hadn't had the practice. The children there had mostly pretended she didn't exist, when they weren't being outright cruel. And on the island, where she was not just the wizard's apprentice but his daughter too, she'd always been surrounded by an impenetrable aura of awe. People didn't know how to reach her through it, and she didn't know how to reach them.

The *Devious* hung heavily from its mooring lines, a phantom ship the color of dusk. Yesterday, Brieze and the wizard had loaded it with supplies and equipment. She tossed her pack full of clothes and personal things into the ship, then turned to face the crowd. But the wizard saved her from having to make her speech right away. He spread his arms wide and recited the benediction for travelers. It was long, and had a lot to do with winds and currents and weather, and also with asking for guidance and protection from ancestors in the realm above. If you believed in that sort of thing. Brieze didn't, and she knew the wizard didn't either. But the words were traditional.

After that, her mother stepped forward. Patentia's nose was red with cold, and her eyes were puffy and pink with crying. She didn't want Brieze to go. They'd done nothing but fight about it since Brieze came up with the idea. But that morning they'd tacitly agreed to a truce. Brieze knew her mother was worried about her safety, but she also suspected her mother was afraid of whatever truth she would bring back from the Eastern Kingdoms.

"Promise me you'll be careful." Patentia squeezed Brieze's hands.

"I promise."

"And be wary of strangers." She squeezed tighter. "You're too trusting."

Brieze huffed and rolled her eyes. "I will mother."

"And stop scowling like that. Nobody likes a scowler."

Brieze made an exasperated grunt in the back of her throat and tried to pull her hands away. But Patentia held on tight to her daughter's hands, then slipped something into them. Something hard and cold. It was the gray heart-shaped stone Kaishou Fujiwara had inscribed. The one she'd tried to throw over the side of the island. "Take it," Patentia whispered. "If you find Kaishou, show it to him. He'll recognize it and know you're telling the truth."

Brieze nodded and stashed the stone in an inner pocket of her flightsuit.

Patentia gave Brieze something else. A heavy drawstring bag, which felt like it might contain marbles, except that it smelled of cinnamon and mint and clove. "Candies," Patentia said. "I know how much you like them. And I know you didn't think to pack any for yourself."

Brieze's eyes glistened. It was just like her mother to be clingy and annoying, and then do something to make her heart flood with gratitude and remember that she loved her. She hugged her mother, hard, and Patentia hugged just as hard back. For a moment, Brieze remembered when it was just the two of them, in their little hut on Footmont. Her mother had been the center of her world then. In all her life, the two of them had never been apart for more than a few days. The realization she would be gone for months and months sank in, and it felt heavy. Patentia began to cry. Brieze felt tears welling up, too. But there was no way she was going to let herself cry in front of that group on the dock. So she stuffed those tears down, disengaged from her mother, and stepped back.

Everyone looked at her expectantly. It was time to make her speech.

She hadn't prepared anything to say. She'd kept putting it off and putting it off, and finally she decided just to wing it. Now, she regretted that decision. She never knew what to say to people. And, somehow, whatever she said always came out wrong.

She cleared her throat. "Well," she said, attempting to sound friendly and informal, "I'm glad at least *some* people showed up to see me off."

Nope. That didn't come out right.

"Not that I expected more people," she hastily added.

They stared at her blankly.

"This is just the right amount of people. I wouldn't have wanted any more or any less."

Some of them shifted uncomfortably. They avoided her eyes.

"What I mean to say is I'm grateful to you all for braving the cold and dark to come see me off."

There, that was better. That was something a normal person would say. She got some approving looks for that.

Unfortunately, that was all she had.

She struggled to come up with more, but all that issued from her throat was a prolonged "Ummmm…uhhhhhhh…

ummmmm," which, as it stretched out into the silence, became a kind of confused, desperate gurgle. It was the kind of
noise that made it seem she wasn't right in the head. Finally,
the unpleasant sound resolved itself into the traditional
"May the winds be kind to you." That was it. That would
have to do. Brieze offered the crowd a wave and what she
hoped was an apologetic smile, but it came out as a funny
little grimace.

"May the winds be kind to you," a few people muttered
back, clearly underwhelmed, offering her grimacy little smile
back to her.

That was all Brieze could stand. She was desperate to get
away. She hopped into the *Devious* and raised the sail. Someone undid the fore and aft mooring lines and gave her a
shove away from the dock. The heavy ship began to sink as
she struggled to get the angle of the sail right. The island
loomed above her like a giant cliff of porous and pitted
stone, with the wooden dock projecting out from it. When
she angled her sail to catch the wind, the *Devious* rose, but
she was so busy with her lines and the tiller and wing flap
pedals that the next time she looked, the island was far
away. It was like a giant slab of stone hanging in the sky,
and the tiny figures waving from the dock were indistinct.

✳   ✳   ✳

Tak sat on the dormitory roof with his cloak wrapped
tightly around his shoulders, cradling a lantern. The sun was
just coming up, tinging the gray sky with morning green. He

should have been in bed with the other cadets. In a matter of minutes, the sergeant would come in and wake them. If the sergeant discovered he wasn't in bed but outside on the roof, it would mean more demerits and pot scrubbing.

He scanned the sky in the direction of the wizard's island. It floated a quarter-mile or so off Selemont, high in the sky, already bright with reflected sun. But Tak's sailspinner ears heard Brieze approach before he saw her. He caught the fluttering rustle of a spider-silk sail, the squeak of a rope being pulled through a cleat, and his eyes darted toward the sound. Heavens! To see Brieze's ship in the sky—or more accurately, to not quite see it—was startling. He saw no hull, no keel, no masts or sail—only vague smudgy glints and shimmers where these things should be. The only thing his eyes detected clearly was the tracery of the ship's rigging against the green morning sky. And the wink of sun reflecting off a metal bracket here and there.

Finally, he caught sight of Brieze herself. Or half of her at least. The top half of her body visible as she sat in the stern with her hand on the tiller. She leaned out over the gunwale and waved with her other hand. Tak leapt to his feet and swung the lantern back and forth. He wished he could leap into the sky! He had to stifle the shout welling up in his throat. It would have wakened the entire dormitory. Possibly the entire academy.

She blew him a kiss.

He blew one back.

And then she was gone. She steered her ship eastward, into the rising sun, and disappeared. A devious girl in an invisible ship, heading into the unknown.

"Watch out Eastern Kingdoms," Tak sighed. "You have no idea what's coming for you."

✳   ✳   ✳

Sitting in the stern of the *Devious* with a hand on the tiller, Brieze sucked on one of the candies her mother had given her, a cinnamon-flavored one, and savored her solitude.

The Highspire Mountains had disappeared below the horizon behind her. There was nothing below her but a sea of silvery-gray clouds, stretching endlessly in every direction. There was nothing above her but sky, and no sign of human beings anywhere—not a glint of sail or wisp of smoke. There was no sound of them, either. None of the unnecessary shouting and constant racket that prevailed on the wizard's island. Brieze sighed contentedly. She was completely, utterly alone! No possibility of anyone watching her, judging her, interrupting her. She felt lighter, freer, than she'd felt in a long time. She breathed the chill air of the Eastern Emptiness deep into her lungs, and it felt invigorating.

She checked her compass and nudged her tiller so the bow of the *Devious* pointed due east.

FIVE

She could never say exactly when it started, but about one month into her voyage, Brieze started talking to herself.

It began with her reminding herself to do things. "It sounded like sleet last night," she said to herself one morning. "You should check the lines for ice." Or, later, "We're listing slightly to port. Maybe you should shift some food stores to the starboard compartments." It seemed harmless enough at first, just a way to fill the silence. But it bothered her because she'd never talked to herself before, and because she had no control over it. She'd resolve to stop, and she'd pop one of her mother's candies into her mouth to keep it busy. She'd suck the candy furiously and roll it around on her tongue. But minutes later the candy was gone, without her even remembering what flavor it had been, and she was doing it again.

"Father warned you about this. He told you people have mental difficulties on long solo voyages."

"I'm not going to go crazy just because I'm alone for a few months. Only a weak-minded person would do that."

"Well shut up then."

The sky had been gray for days, and the grayness wore on her spirit. She missed the cheery morning green, the deep noon blue, and the serene evening lavender of Etherium's usual sky. The gray clouds above merged with the gray surface clouds below so that the horizon disappeared. The *Devious* became a ghostly gray ship floating in a gray void. It was hard for Brieze to even tell that she was moving. The Eastern Emptiness. She hadn't realized how true that name was until now. She longed to see a mountain, a bird, any sign of life—but she knew it would be more than another month yet. The gray sky offered her only cold rain and freezing sleet. Gusts of wind sawed at her rigging over and over again like the bow of a maniacal violinist, making each taut, quivering rope whimper and moan.

She'd taken to spending more and more time in the ship's weather shelter—a kind of tent rigged up between the fore and aft masts, with flaps at the front and back. Such shelters were standard gear for long-distance, cold-weather traveling. Inside the shelter were the ship's two thwart benches with her sleeping bag laid out between them, a lantern, and her personal odds and ends. She sat on one of the benches, carefully emptied the candy bag into her palm, and counted them. There had been fifty when she started.

There were thirteen left.

She counted again just to make sure. Thirteen.

She did a quick calculation in her head. With a month and a half left in her voyage, that came to 0.28888 candies per day.

"No point in rationing them anymore. Might as well finish them off."

"What are you going to do when they're gone?"

She shrugged.

"Can you stand a month-and-a-half more of this?"

She shrugged again.

"You could turn around and head home. Right now. You could try again in the spring. Go with your father, like he suggested. And maybe Tak, too."

She popped a candy into her mouth and considered.

"Nope," she said, rolling the butterscotch-flavored ball around on her tongue. "No turning back." She imagined the looks on their faces if she returned home without finishing the journey, defeated by nothing more than her own loneliness. She'd rather perish in the Eastern Emptiness than endure that humiliation.

"Get a grip on yourself then. You're starting to lose it."

She took several deep breaths. "Okay," she said. "I've got a grip. I'm good."

She was carefully transferring the candies back to the bag when the ship lurched with a gust of wind and they spilled out of her palm. They went bouncing and skittering and rolling in every direction, disappearing into every corner and crevice of the ship.

Brieze shrieked. Tears welled up in her eyes.

She spent the next several hours on her hands and knees, crawling around the ship, hunting candies.

✳   ✳   ✳

In another couple of weeks, Brieze started to hear things. She spent almost all her time inside the weather shelter now. The lantern-lit space inside its canvas walls was small and manageable. The world outside, with its endless clouds and sky, was too big, too empty and overwhelming. She went out there only when necessary. She'd run out of candies, but she held onto the drawstring bag. Whenever she craved one, she stuck her nose into the bag and breathed deeply, sighing at the faint aromas of cinnamon and mint.

She'd taken to lying on her sleeping bag for hours at a time, stroking her long braid. She'd pull it over her shoulder, curl her hands around it, and run them along its length, first one hand, then the other, over and over, enjoying its knotty texture against her palms. It was a soothing habit she'd acquired in childhood. Holding onto her braid, Brieze felt a connection to her mother. Her mother had started braiding her hair when she was little, and she'd taught Brieze how to do it when she got older.

She listened to the sounds of the ship. The spider silk sail fluttered and snapped as the wind shifted. Ropes creaked as they stretched taut and slackened. An empty water cask in one of the storage compartments rolled back and forth, back and forth, as the ship rocked. And Brieze swore she still heard that last candy rolling around somewhere. She'd dropped twelve of them, but only recovered eleven. One was still hiding aboard the ship, rolling around, taunting her. She'd looked everywhere for it. Then she looked everywhere again. She'd unpacked and searched every storage compartment. She'd spent hours on her hands and knees, probing every nook and crevice of the ship with her fingers.

As her ears strained to locate that rolling candy, they caught a new sound.

The deck creaked as if someone were walking around outside.

Yes! There it was again. Definitely footsteps.

Someone else was aboard the *Devious*.

And instantly, Brieze knew who it was. It was Tak. He had wanted to come with her. Somehow, he'd managed to stow himself aboard unseen. And now, he was sneaking around outside. He probably wanted to show himself, but he was hesitating because he knew she'd be angry with him. That would be just like him. Except she wouldn't be angry. She desperately wanted to see him. She would throw her arms around him and kiss him. Kiss him a lot.

"Tak is *not* out there," the more sensible part of her said. "You're pathologically lonely and you're hearing things."

"It wouldn't hurt to look," she answered.

She poked her head out of the rear flaps of the weather shelter. There was no one in the stern of the ship. The stern seat was empty. The tiller was still tied there, keeping the ship on its easterly course. The wing flap pedals were in neutral position.

The deck creaked again. From the bow!

Brieze dashed around, scrambled over the thwart benches, and stuck her head out the front flaps of the weather shelter.

She screamed with shock and joy.

Tak was there! Standing right there on the bow deck, grinning at her. His brown hair and lanky arms waved in the wind.

Except it wasn't Tak…it was just her cloak, which she'd hung from the bowsprit stay. It had gotten soaked with rain, and she'd hung it there hoping it would dry. Its empty hood and arms flapped in the wind.

She closed her eyes and took a deep breath. "If you don't do something soon, you're going to go completely off the deep end."

"What can I do? I need to talk to someone. But there's no one around for hundreds and hundreds of miles."

She chewed her lower lip and thought about that.

An idea came to her.

"Letters!" she said. "You could write letters."

She pulled her head back inside the weather shelter. She dug through her pack and found her paper and ink, her envelopes and wax. She arranged these on one of the benches. She turned up the lantern so it burned brighter.

"They won't get these letters for a long time, but they will get them. They'll read them one day. So this will be like talking to them."

For the next several hours, Brieze wrote letters. Her quill scratched against the paper, plunged into the jar of ink, scratched again. She wrote Tak first. A long letter. A letter unlike any she'd ever written. She told him over and over again how much she missed him, and she said a lot of other things she would never have said under ordinary circumstances. Romantic, mushy, tender things. It felt good to say them. It made her heart beat a little faster, her breath quicken.

After that, she wrote to her mother and her wizard father. When the letters were finished, she addressed them and sealed them with wax. Her hand ached from all the writing. The sun had set. Brieze doused the lantern and crawled into her sleeping bag. She held the letters to her chest, and she fell asleep to the gentle rocking of the ship with a contented smile on her face.

SIX

A ship!

Brieze and the *Devious* were overtaking a merchant ship—large and heavy, clearly from the Eastern Kingdoms by the square shape of its sails and the lines of its hull, and heading back from somewhere west. Brieze blinked and rubbed her eyes to make sure she wasn't hallucinating.

It was real!

This was good. It confirmed she was on the right course.

"Hail them! Talk to them! Find out where they're going!" she said to herself.

But as starved as she was for human company, something made her hesitate. A reluctance, a fear, that was difficult to put into words. She knew that women were treated differently in the East. They weren't allowed to serve on airships. Eastern airmen were extremely superstitious, and they considered a woman on a voyage to be bad luck. What would they think of her, a young woman appearing out of nowhere in a strangely invisible airship, half-crazed with loneliness? What if they told her to go away, to get lost?

"I couldn't bear that," she said.

She decided, for the time being, to just stick close and watch them. With the *Devious* taking on the color of the sky, she could approach closely without being spotted. Close enough to make out every detail of the ship, and even the faces of the crewmen, through her spyglass. Like many merchant ships, it flew by sail alone, without the heaviness of steel boilers and propellers, which allowed it to carry more cargo. It was weighed down with freight, riding the currents with a ponderous rising and falling, every sail hoisted and straining to keep it aloft. The ship was lightly armed, with only a few small cannon mounted in the bow and stern, although she saw racks of spears, shields, and cutlasses along the gunwales.

It was strange to see so many faces with Eastern features like her own. Raven-black hair. Almond-shaped eyes. The captain of the ship was tall, and he wore a very long, elaborately plaited black beard, the end of which he tucked into his broad belt. He usually stood on the command deck, gazing anxiously eastward, stroking his beard. Or he strode the decks from bow to stern, shouting orders, the tails of his greatcoat flapping in the wind.

At night, Brieze stole in closer—so close she heard the creaking of the ships' wooden beams and the men calling to each other. She could make out a few of the words. She caught whiffs of their dinner cooking, the scent of exotic spices she had no names for. And after dinner the men lit colored paper lanterns, strung them up in the rigging, and sang. Sometimes the singing was light and cheery, other times slow and mournful. The melodies, with their odd notes and dips and lilts, were at once strange and familiar. They stirred up odd feelings in Brieze, and things that were like memories, but memories she never knew she had, of places she'd never been. They filled her with an intense longing to be *home*. But not her old home on Footmont or her new home on the wizard's island.

Some other home.

Where was that?

*   *   *

On the third night that she traveled unseen in their company, something happened to bring Brieze closer to these strange yet familiar men.

She saved their lives.

The night was calm. The sky was clear. The stars were scattered from horizon to horizon overhead, burning brightly, without a cloud or mountain peak anywhere to blot them. The men on the ship lit their colored lanterns and sang a cheerful song. The lanterns attracted strange glowing creatures from the depths of the night. There were little pink ones that buzzed and darted among the lanterns. The men paid them little mind. Some of these creatures sensed the *Devious* in the darkness, though the ship showed no lights. They flitted curiously about. One landed for a moment on the gunwale near Brieze. It looked like a cross between a shrimp and a dragonfly. Its two pairs of wings whirred. Its glowing pink crustacean tail and antennae twitched. It darted off, joining its fellows.

The pink creatures attracted something else—a school of ghostly, glimmering aerial octopi. Brieze had come across these creatures before, but never so many at once! She knew them to be gentle, harmless, intelligent even. Their bodies were mottled with a bluish-green bioluminescence, in a pattern like camouflage. Their pulsing, balloon-like heads were about the size of her own. Their eyes glistened, and, as they floated all around her, their long tentacles slithered sinuously and mesmerizingly on the night breeze, like something out of a dream.

The stars, the music, the strange beauty of the nighttime creatures—Brieze leaned back and breathed in the enchantment of it all. The comforting melody of the song and gentle rocking of her ship lulled her into a peaceful doze. Her eyes closed. She smiled.

And then something changed. The men's singing stopped abruptly. Brieze's eyes snapped open. The pink creatures and the octopi had disappeared. The men called to each other in urgent whispers and extinguished the lanterns and all other lights on their ship.

A nasty smell like rotting fish wafted on the night air.

Brieze's heart thumped and her throat tightened. She knew what that stench meant—Nagmor. The depths of the Eastern Emptiness were filled with nighttime predators, but the biggest, scariest, and least studied and understood of these were the Nagmor. Brieze had read everything there was to read about them, which wasn't much. In the old language, the name translated literally into "night death." The gigantic creatures were capable of overwhelming a ship and crushing it to pieces. And they smelled worse than anything in Etherium. Other than that, not a lot was known about them. Few who encountered them lived to report back. No one had ever gotten close enough to study one in any detail.

Brieze sensed as much as she saw the creature behind them—an expanding splotch of denser darkness in the night sky, blotting out the stars. It was big, and approaching fast. The merchant vessel, completely lightless now, drifted passively on the current. It was as still and quiet as a large airship like that could be. Brieze nudged the tiller of the *Devious* and kept pace with the ship, floating a few lengths off their starboard side. The Nagmor came up close behind the merchant ship, also keeping pace with it. The creature seemed to be studying the vessel, considering whether or not it might be prey. It was difficult to tell in the darkness, but the beast and ship seemed about the same size. The Nagmor's putrid reek grew so powerful it watered Brieze's eyes. She felt it like a tickle in the back of her throat.

Most airship captains faced with a Nagmor approaching from behind would have tried to veer away and make a run for it. But that would have been a mistake. Acting like prey would have only triggered the animal's hunting and killing instinct. And Nagmor can move faster than any airship. The merchant vessel's captain didn't flinch. Didn't make a move. He just allowed his ship to drift as the creature drew closer.

The Nagmor dove beneath the ship, passed underneath it, fast as the wind, creating a wave that made the ship bob and toss. Brieze thought that maybe they were safe now, that the beast decided to pass them by. But the creature rose up, ahead of them now. More quickly than she would have thought possible, it turned in the air. In the moonlight and starlight, she could make out suggestions of its long body, bulbous head, and grasping tentacles as it flew straight at the merchant vessel.

Still, the captain didn't flinch. He maintained his course. He appeared to be betting the safety of his ship and the lives of his crew on the not-acting-like-prey idea. He seemed to be hoping that, if he played a game of chicken with the beast, it might swerve first and leave them alone. The two light cannons in the bow, which had been silently and stealthily loaded, fired. After all the darkness and silence, the flash and crack of the cannons made Brieze blink and jump. The shots must have hit—the Nagmor was at point blank range and closing fast—but the beast didn't swerve or slow down.

With a tremendous crunch, ship and animal crashed together.

The ship came alive with noise and light. Men cried out as they were knocked off their feet and scrambled to regain their footing. They lit torches and lanterns. Distress flares shot into the sky, though who the men expected to see them Brieze couldn't guess. The flares trailed orange sparks and glowed a phosphorescent red, hanging in the sky and casting an eerie light on the scene.

Brieze saw the Nagmor more clearly in the glow of the flares. Its cone-shaped body tapered to a pointed tail with a wing-like fin—or was it a fin-like wing?—on either side. A roundish head bulged from the wide end of the cone, with glassy black eyes. Nasty-looking tentacles covered with suckers and spines sprouted from the head. The tentacles rimmed a gaping mouth lined with spiky, inward-pointing teeth. The mouth clamped down on the bow of the merchant ship. Teeth dug into the wooden beams. Tentacles thick as tree trunks slithered across the deck, coiling around and squeezing whatever they could find. Men screamed horribly. Masts cracked and splintered. Taut ropes snapped and whistled in the air.

Everywhere, men hacked at the tentacles with cutlasses and stabbed them with spears. The Nagmor made deep, filthy grunting sounds as if in pain, but otherwise the blows had no effect. The beast's mouth bit down harder on the bow of the ship, and the planks there began to warp and crack. The captain stood on the forward deck, facing the creature. He drew his cutlass and brandished it, shouting for his men to gather around him. Some of them did. They appeared to be readying themselves to charge directly into the mouth of the beast.

Brieze watched, frozen with horror and fascination. But she snapped herself out of it as she realized she could help these men. Her wizard father had loaded the *Devious* with an arsenal of devices and weapons to help her out of any danger she might encounter. In other words, a *lot* of stuff. What leapt to her mind were the bombs. Unique bombs containing an explosive the wizard had invented himself, ten times more powerful than gunpowder. The bombs looked like nothing more than black, egg-shaped lumps of iron, with a short fuse at the small end. They fit comfortably in her hand. The wizard had instructed her in their use, thinking they would be ideal for repelling a pirate attack.

"If a pirate ship draws close enough, toss one or two of

these onto its deck," he'd said. "That will take care of them."

Brieze rummaged through her gear and brought out two of the bombs. Her nimble mind was forming a plan. Simply tossing the bombs at the Nagmor would do no good. They would probably just bounce off the creature's thick skin and blow her and the merchant ship to bits. But if she could get one down the beast's throat, *that* would do some damage.

To get a bomb down its throat, though, she'd have to throw from close range, and at the correct angle.

In other words, from the deck of the merchant ship itself. From about where the captain and his men were standing, readying themselves to charge.

Brieze's mind worked fast in tight situations. So fast she was hardly aware of it, she just moved, acted. She angled her sail, leaned on her tiller, pressed the wing flap pedals, and banked the *Devious* into a tight turn, aiming for the ship's rigging—the complicated system of ropes, stays, and ratlines that ran from the deck and gunwales up to the masts and yards and sails. She crashed into the rigging on purpose. The *Devious* sliced through some of the ropes, but others caught and held the ship as if it were a bird tangled up in a net. That would keep it close and prevent it from drifting off. The *Devious* leaned at a crazy angle. Brieze unclipped her lifeline, lit the fuses of the two bombs, and jumped from the deck with one in each hand, aiming straight for the captain and the knot of men gathering on the foredeck. She spread her arms and legs wide—the wings of her flightsuit snapped taught as they caught the wind. It was hard to control her descent with a heavy, burning bomb in each hand. She veered and wobbled, but she managed…

* * *

What the men on the merchant ship saw, each of them sure he was about to die, was a winged figure in black descending on them from above. Its hands glowed with fire, trailing sparks. The thing landed among them, knocking some down, scattering the others.

"Back!" the figure cried. "Get back!"

The apparition gathered itself up and strode right up to the mouth of the beast. It hurled one bit of fire down the beast's throat. Then the other. Both disappeared. And then, for the space of a few heartbeats, nothing happened.

With a guttural bellow that shook every plank of the ship, the Nagmor erupted. It exploded into several large pieces, scatting its awful innards in every direction—the bones of old ships and devoured crew, chunks of prey that had been rotting inside it for untold time, other pieces of filth too bizarre to name or describe.

The tail of the beast spun away into the darkness. The head remained intact, mouth still gripping the bow. But the mouth had gone slack. Tentacles flopped limply to the deck. With a grating of sharp, spiked teeth against wood, the giant head slipped away from the bow and fell into the darkness below, snapping the bowsprit and dragging its lifeless tentacles with it.

* * *

For a long time, nobody said anything. Everyone was too dazed with shock, with fear, with relief, with the incomprehensible reek of the beast all around them. The men gathered in a loose knot around Brieze. They looked at her. They looked at each other. She stood doubled over, hands on her knees, trying to get her breath back but at the same time trying not to breathe too deeply for fear of being overcome by the stench.

The wind whistled through the rigging. The wounded ship groaned.

And then, one by one, the men knelt and bowed their heads. Some got down on all fours and pressed their foreheads to the deck. They murmured fearfully but excitedly among themselves. Brieze caught a word here and there. *Tenshi*. Angel. *Kami*. Divine being.

The captain knelt, but on one knee only. He bowed his head slightly, keeping his eyes on Brieze. He was not as superstitious as his crew. His mind tended to rational, not supernatural, explanations of things. Still, an awed expression softened the rough features of his bearded, weather-beaten face. He knew he was in the presence of something very much out of the ordinary.

"Whatever you are," he said in the Eastern language, "*whoever* you are, we are grateful to you beyond words. We owe you our lives. My ship, my crew, and I are at your service."

Brieze straightened up, caught her breath, and began to stammer. Her hands shook with adrenaline. "I'm not an angel. I'm just…just a girl." Few of the men appeared to understand her, so she repeated this in the Eastern language.

The captain arched an eyebrow skeptically. He noted her preference for the Western tongue and responded in kind, speaking fluently. "Just a girl? A girl who appears out of nowhere, flies on her own wings, and destroys the beast that my crew and I could not? Are you sure that you are really *just* a girl?"

"Well," Brieze said, and a little smile crooked the corner of her mouth. She couldn't help feeling flattered, "I *am* a wizard's apprentice." She repeated the phrase in the eastern tongue.

The men looked to one another, comprehension dawning on their faces. The captain nodded. That explanation made some sense to him. But the men remained kneeling. Brieze could tell by the looks and whispers that passed among them that while a wizard's apprentice might not be an angel or divine being, it was close enough in most of their books.

"My name is Brieze. Apprentice to the wizard Radolphus of the Kingdom of Spire in the West."

The captain stood and offered her a formal bow. "I am Captain Hiroshi of the city of Kyo. This ship is called the *Kinzou*. My crew and I are at your service. Is there something we can do to repay you for your kindness and bravery? Ask anything you wish. If it is in my power to grant, I will."

"Well…" Brieze cocked her eye up at the ship's rigging. "You could help me get my ship out of your rigging."

"Ship?" Captain Hiroshi squinted, following her gaze. "I see no ship up there."

Brieze smiled. There was a thing or two she would have to explain to these men.

SEVEN

In the hours immediately after the Nagmor attack, there was little time for Brieze to explain anything. Captain Hiroshi's first order of business was to keep the *Kinzou* from sinking. The first of its four tall, strong masts had been snapped by the Nagmor's squeezing tentacles, and the second had been badly cracked and splintered. The ship could no longer carry enough sail to keep itself aloft. It was losing altitude at an alarming rate, sinking nose-down. Hiroshi asked that Brieze remain at his side until he had dealt with this problem. She agreed, but it was difficult to do, as the man was everywhere at once, striding from one end of his ship to the other and shouting orders to the crew as they made frantic repairs.

Some of the crew disentangled the *Devious* from the rigging. Once they'd gotten over boggling at its properties of color, the captain asked if they could tie the *Devious* to his own ship's sagging bow. Even the small lift its sail could provide would help, he said. Brieze agreed. A new bowsprit was quickly rigged and the *Devious* was lashed to it with sturdy rope. The warped and cracked bow planks were hammered back into place and patched up as best the crew could.

A much shorter and weaker temporary spare mast replaced the snapped foremast. And the second cracked mast was bolstered and braced. Sails were quickly raised on these masts, but not nearly as much sail as the originals could have carried. On the good masts, sail yards were lengthened by tying on extra lengths of wood to their ends. Extra sail was stitched on, riggers working furiously while hanging precariously from harnesses.

While all this was going on, some crew members scrubbed the decks, trying to remove the Nagmor's terrible stench.

All these repairs and riggings were not enough. The *Kinzou* was still too heavy. Its nose straightened out, but it continued to lose altitude, though at a much slower rate. The ship creaked and complained. Every squeaking rope threatened to give up and snap.

Captain Hiroshi announced they would have to toss some cargo.

The crew groaned in dismay.

"Quit your belly aching!" Hiroshi shouted. "I don't like it any better than you. But do you want to get home alive, or would you rather be ghosts wandering and wailing beneath the clouds?"

The men got to work.

The *Kinzou* had sailed to the Kingdom of Spire with its holds full of rice, silk, tea, and spices. The captain had traded these for a commodity the west had plenty of, but which had grown rare and precious in the east—wood. The ship's cargo holds were filled with tightly packed, heavy pine trunks that had been felled by lumberjacks in the Dragonback mountains. This timber was destined for the capital city of Kyo, where it would be sawed into lumber. Some of it would be used to replace the old, rotting wooden doors and window frames of the city's stone houses, but most of it would be used to build new airships. The Eastern Kingdoms always needed more airships.

The captain and crew of the *Kinzou* would make a tremendous profit on the timber they carried. Every tree they tossed would lessen that profit.

The main deck's cargo hatch was opened. Teams of men hauled up the heavy pine trunks and heaved them overboard. Captain Hiroshi ordered that they be thrown overboard one at a time, and he looked up at the sails and gauged the effect before allowing another to be jettisoned. He looked miserable as he did this, like he was in physical pain, as if he were giving up teeth to a dentist's pliers.

Brieze, standing at his elbow, felt the urge to comfort him. "It's just wood," she said. "There's plenty more where that came from."

Hiroshi sighed. "Where I come from, every one of those trees is worth its weight in silver."

Brieze chewed on that for a while.

"Still," he said. "We are alive thanks to you. And we might yet reach home safely. And there will still be profit." He closed his eyes, breathed slowly and calmly, and folded his hands into a contemplative pose. "So all is well. I am grateful."

When about a quarter of the cargo had been dumped, the captain judged they were light enough to get back to Kyo. And so with every sail and rope straining, the *Kinzou* made its slow, aching journey home.

* * *

Brieze spent the remainder of her journey to the Eastern Kingdoms aboard the *Kinzou* as a guest, getting to know the ship, its crew, and especially its captain. Hiroshi had more or less begged her to stay with them. "My men would feel… safer if you continued with us on our journey," he'd said, and added with a hopeful smile, "and I confess that I would, too."

Brieze didn't take much convincing. She didn't want to go back to talking to herself in the gray void of the Eastern Emptiness. She'd felt a bond with these men the first time she heard them singing by the light of their colored lanterns at night, and she didn't want to break it. And travelling with them would give her the opportunity to sharpen her language skills and learn more about the strange culture she was about to immerse herself in, she told herself.

She'd planned on sleeping in the weather shelter aboard the *Devious*, but the captain insisted that she use his cabin. He bunked in the hammocks with his officers. The tiny cabin was the only sleeping quarters on the ship with a real bed, though a small one with a thin mat instead of a mattress, and a window that looked out from the stern of the ship.

Hiroshi also insisted that she dine with him in the cabin each evening, at a table that folded out from the wall. The meal was most often flying fish, heavily salted but prepared in a variety of delicious ways, with rice. Sometimes, when the crew could catch food, the fare was more exotic—a jellyfish stew or roasted octopus. With a little instruction from Hiroshi, Brieze grew adept at using the two sticks Easterners used for utensils, instead of forks or spoons.

"What is this flavor I'm tasting?" Brieze asked at their first dinner, closing her eyes and savoring a bite of fish. "It's sweet, but nutty." Flying fish was frequently eaten in the west, but it was usually fried or baked, and bland.

Hiroshi smiled. "That would be coconut," he said. "We get them from the south, and we simmer the fish in their juice."

"Coconut?" Brieze said. "I never heard of it."

"I'll have the cook give you one," he said.

She decided to tell Hiroshi the reason for her journey, although she left out the details of what she planned to do when she met her biological father. She trusted the captain, and he seemed like someone who could help and advise her. He listened gravely to her story. His eyes widened at the mention of the name Fujiwara. "The Fujiwaras are a numerous and powerful clan," he said. "They essentially rule the city of Kyo and the mountains of Onshu while the Emperor keeps to himself in the north. I do not know specifically of a man named Kaishou Fujiwara, but Kaishou is a common name and there might be several Kaishou Fujiwaras in

Kyo."

"How can I find the right one?" Brieze asked.

Hiroshi grinned. "When we get to Kyo, the story of how you saved us from the beast will make you famous. You'll be a celebrity. I'm sure the leaders of the Fujiwara clan will want to meet you, and they will know where your Kaishou is. I can make the arrangements for the meeting."

Brieze thanked him, but inwardly she felt troubled. Her business with Kaishou Fujiwara was a private matter, and she wanted it to be a secret. She had thought to slip unnoticed into the city of Kyo, discover the whereabouts of the man, and confront him. She didn't like the idea of arriving in the city as a celebrity and having everyone know her business.

The captain's next words troubled her further. "I will give you some advice. The Fujiwaras are powerful and proud. They hold their family honor dear. If this Kaishou Fujiwara did as you said, then he acted dishonorably. If you were to meet with them and bluntly accuse them of this dishonor, it would not go well. I urge you to be more… diplomatic."

"I have some experience with diplomacy," Brieze said.

"And another thing. The Fujiwaras are a scheming lot. They're always looking to increase their power and advance their interests. If they can figure out a way to use you for their own ends, they will. So be careful. Don't become a pawn in one of their games. Be wary. They can be quite… devious."

"Devious," Brieze smiled wryly. "That *sounds* like my

family."

*　*　*

One evening Brieze leaned her elbows on the aft deck rail of the *Kinzou* and watched the sun set in the evening lavender of the western sky. As the sun's disc touched the horizon, it seemed to set the surface clouds afire. They burned with that special pinkish-orange glow that only the setting sun creates.

A lookout called something she didn't quite catch, and men began to exclaim and call to each other throughout the ship. She turned. Everyone gazed and pointed at something on the eastern horizon ahead of them. A crowd gathered on the forward deck. She moved through the crowd—every man stepped back to give her room and offered her a deferential bow. She smiled and nodded back. She stood in the prow of the ship and looked.

The eastern horizon was already dark as night. But she spotted what seemed like fire there, too. Flickers and sparkles of red and orange, as if there were tremendously tall mountains ahead and huge bonfires had been lit on their peaks. She guessed what they must be, and a little thrill ran through her.

Hiroshi came to her side and confirmed her guess. "The Wind's Teeth," he said. "The rays of the setting sun are just catching their peaks. We should reach them tomorrow, shortly after sunrise."

Brieze had read all about The Wind's Teeth and had

heard the countless stories. They were *the* greatest natural wonder in all of Etherium, nothing else came close—a beautiful and strange, dazzling and dangerous geological formation.

"I was going to fly around them," she said. "I don't have the skill to navigate them on my own. What are you going to do?"

Hiroshi stroked his beard. "It takes two or three weeks to go around, but only one day to go through," he said. "So I will take the risk. Our pace is slow. We've lost much time and can't afford to lose any more."

"Wow," Brieze's eyes sparkled. "I can't believe I'm going to see them up close, and actually go through them!"

Hiroshi grinned wryly. "Spoken like a true wizard's apprentice and Nagmor-slayer," he said. "I myself, who have been through them many times, am not quite so enthusiastic."

✳   ✳   ✳

In the dawn light, The Wind's Teeth stood before them—taller than any mountains by far and much thinner and sharper. To Brieze, who'd been waiting for a first glimpse of them in the prow of the *Kinzou* since before sunup, they at first looked like a forest of glittering crystalline stalagmites holding up the roof of the sky. The next moment, they looked to her like a vast shimmering field of upside-down icicles. But she could see now how they got their name. They also looked like rows of ragged fangs protruding from the lower jaw of some impossibly huge creature, a creature that could swallow entire worlds with a single bite.

The Teeth stretched far away to the north and south, sparkling like diamonds in the morning sun.

The *Kinzou* aimed for a small gap that marked the middle passage. Hiroshi took the wheel and steered the ship himself. He called orders to the knots of crewmen who worked the ropes to trim the sails. As they entered the middle passage and nosed along it, the Teeth closed in behind them, and the wind grew rougher and less predictable. That was one of the tricks the Teeth played with the wind. They forced the big trade currents to break up into smaller currents that twisted and turned as they slithered through whatever gaps they could find. Sometimes the currents looped and eddied and turned back on themselves, forming whirlpools or windspouts.

Brieze stood in her privileged spot at the captain's side. It was hard for her to keep her sense of direction. She couldn't see the sun, and wherever she looked the view was the same—mind-boggling huge spires of crystal scattered in every direction, with only small slivers of sky visible between their sharp peaks. But Hiroshi kept a close eye on the compass in the binnacle, and he seemed to know where he was going.

The Teeth played another trick with the wind. As it was forced through crevices and cracks and narrow passages, the wind whistled and howled and moaned. Somehow the sounds were both otherworldly, like the mutterings of a giant made of stone, and strangely human and voice like.

Groups of crewmen who were not on duty gathered at the rails and listened with bowed heads. Soon, they began to sing together. A gentle song, as if they were trying to calm the wind.

"What are they doing?" Brieze asked Hiroshi.

"They believe those sounds are the wailings of ghosts of men who have wrecked here," Hiroshi said. "Their song is supposed to appease the restless spirits and ask for safe passage."

"There's no such thing as ghosts," Brieze said.

"I would agree," said Hiroshi. "But my men are right about one thing. There is a vast graveyard of ships down there under the clouds among the roots of the Teeth. More wrecks than anywhere on Etherium, and especially along the middle passage." Seeing Brieze frown, Hiroshi hastened to reassure her. "Not because the middle passage is any more dangerous than the others. Simply because it is the one most travelled."

Brieze thought about that. She had journeyed beneath the surface clouds once, on a diplomatic mission to the Gublins, and she knew what it was like down there. She imagined the bones of long-dead airmen and the hulks of broken ships rotting in the stifling dark and dampness, where the sun cast the barest glimmer of light through a heavy fog. The image made her shiver.

"When will we pass through?" she asked. The wind picked up and whipped her long braid back and forth, despite the weight on its end. She grabbed the braid and held onto it; stroked it as if trying to soothe a frightened cat. The

Kinzou bobbed and rocked ponderously on the wind.

"If we're not out before sunset, we'll be in worlds of trouble," he said. "You can't navigate the Teeth in the dark." He looked anxiously up at the sails. Nothing grew on the Wind's Teeth, not a single tree or blade of grass. There were no birds or other creatures either. The place was barren. So captains couldn't read the currents the way they usually did, by studying the swaying branches on a mountainside or the swirling pattern of a flock of birds. The only warning they would have of a rogue current or windspout about to strike would be a brief luffing and chattering of the sails before it hit them.

Minute by minute and hour by hour, the *Kinzou* inched its way along the middle passage, a kind of long gap or valley that snaked through the Teeth. The sun climbed until it shone directly down on them above the peaks, then it edged past noon toward the western horizon and evening. The crew was quiet, their faces tense as they went about their business. No midday meal had been served. No one had any appetite. Except Brieze that is. Her stomach rumbled hungrily. But she ignored it, coughing or clearing her throat to cover the sound. Hiroshi didn't notice. His attention was focused on the passage ahead, and the wind. He never left his post at the wheel, never even took his hands off it.

A lookout broke the silence. "Sail behind!" he called.

Hiroshi gritted his teeth, but he didn't take his eyes off the way ahead to look behind them. "Of course," he snarled.

"What does that mean?" Brieze asked.

"Pirates," he said.

Brieze had read that several bands of pirates lurked in the Teeth. They especially liked to prey on distressed or damaged ships. They hid out in the crystalline caves that bored like cavities into the Teeth, far from the armies and authorities of lawful nations. She climbed a little way up a nearby set of ratlines, took out her spyglass, and gazed through it. The ship behind them was little more than a dark silhouette against the glassy shimmering of the Teeth.

"I don't think it's a pirate ship," she said.

"Why not?" Hiroshi asked.

"It looks like a Western ship. From what I can see, it's built like one of the ships of Spire's royal fleet."

"You think Westerners can't be pirates?"

Brieze climbed down from the ratlines. She was about to say *yes*, but realized that was just prejudice on her part. To her, pirates were always bad men from *other* places. She didn't like to think that men from her own country could turn criminal.

"Pirates come from every corner of Etherium, even your proud West," Hiroshi said, guessing her thoughts. "If that were a lawful ship plying the eastern current we would have seen her before we entered the middle passage. Lawful ships don't suddenly appear behind you among the Teeth, but pirates have a nasty habit of doing just that."

"Will they attack?" Brieze asked.

"Hard to say. They're sure to see we're damaged. They'll probably just skulk back there, hoping we run into some trouble they can take advantage of. That's their usual way. But if they're desperate, or more aggressive they might—"

He was interrupted by a sound like a huge angry hornet buzzing by over their heads. They both ducked instinctively. Brieze had never heard that sound before, but she instantly recognized it—a cannon ball zooming past.

Hiroshi swore eloquently in the Eastern tongue. Beads of sweat broke out on his forehead. "Damn them! It's hard enough to navigate here without having to take evasive maneuvers." But he spun the wheel, and the *Kinzou* did its best to dance upon the wind, bobbing and drifting up and down, and side to side, to evade more shots, even as it crept forward.

"Can't we shoot back?" Brieze asked, swaying to keep her feet.

"Their cannons are bigger than ours. They'll stay out of our range and lob long-distance shots at us, hoping to get lucky and hit something."

Another shot whizzed by, snapping the portside stay of the aft mast. Crewmen rushed to repair the damage.

"Ever been attacked by pirates before?"

"I've had a few close calls. Once when I was a lad, on my grandfather's ship, pirates tried to board us."

"What happened?"

Hiroshi was quiet for a moment. "I'd rather not talk about it," he said.

Brieze hadn't been truly afraid until Hiroshi said that. She didn't ask any more questions. Her mouth clamped shut, and it didn't want to move. For the next half-hour, the *Kinzou* crawled along the middle passage, its deck pitching as Hiroshi did his best to evade the cannon shots. None hit, but with each buzzing ball that tore past them or over their heads the knots in Brieze's belly tightened, until they were so tight she could barely breathe.

The lookout shouted something so fast and high-pitched Brieze didn't catch it.

Hiroshi swore again. "They're moving in. We're almost through the Teeth, and they know it. They're going to try for us before we can get out to open sky and escape."

Brieze heard the *Kinzou's* stern cannons fire. The shots were answered by a shot from the pirate ship that hit the *Kinzou* somewhere aft. She felt it in the soles of her feet, and heard wood shattering and splintering. White smoke and the sulfurous reek of gunpowder thickened the air. Men were shouting. It seemed unreal to her, that she should suddenly be caught in the middle of an airship battle. She never imagined anything like this would happen on her journey. She tried to think of what she could do to help.

She and Hiroshi got the same idea at the same time.

"Got any of those bombs left?" he asked, arching an eyebrow.

Brieze smiled. "I was about to fetch them."

"You see?" he gave her a brave, sweaty smile in return, and winked. "I feel safer already."

Brieze hurried forward to the bow. She climbed up the bowsprit with catlike agility. The *Devious* had been tightly lashed there, with strong ropes that coiled around its bow and stern. The ropes were so tight the *Devious* barely moved, but its small sail was full and straining with wind, doing its part to keep the *Kinzou* aloft. Brieze climbed into her ship and rummaged through its compartments. She found two bombs and tucked them into inner pockets of her cloak. As she climbed out of the *Devious* and prepared to make her way back down the bowsprit, a sound above her caught her attention. She looked up.

The *Devious's* small sail was luffing and chattering.

A moment later, so was every sail on the *Kinzou*.

Captain Hiroshi's voice boomed, at a level of volume Brieze hadn't known was humanly possible, "*All hands, brace yourselves!*"

She had just enough time to jump back into the *Devious*, wrap her arms around the aft mast, and hook her feet under a thwart bench.

With a rushing roar it hit them—a rising, swirling spout of wind, incredibly strong. There was a loud whoof as every sail snapped taut and strained to the breaking point, the masts creaked, and the heavy merchant ship lifted and swirled about as if it were nothing more than a dry autumn leaf. The ship rocked and yawed violently. Hiroshi shouted for help as he wrestled with the wheel to keep the ship from capsizing. Several crewmen rushed to his aid. As the *Kinzou* rose higher and higher, the stony flanks of nearby Teeth rushed past them, some veering terrifyingly close. Men were swept overboard, looking like so much dandelion fluff as their parachutes opened and they whirled helplessly with the current.

When the *Kinzou* had been lifted so high that the air was thin and bitterly cold, the windspout died. The ship spun lazily about, and finally came to a halt. The rocking and yawing settled into a stable drift.

Brieze loosened her grip ever so slightly on the *Devious's* mast and sat there, dizzy and shaken. She tried to gather her scattered wits. Men were shouting and calling to each other all over the ship. Crewmen on parachutes were returning, landing and rolling and kissing the wooden planks, accompanied by the cheers of their comrades.

Brieze shivered violently. Her breath came out in white puffs of steam. It was *cold*. The lining of her nose froze every time she breathed in, and it was hard to get enough air. When her head had stopped spinning and she felt sufficiently nimble, she climbed down the bowsprit and reached the forward deck. It was all shouting and confusion and men bumping into each other as they ran this way and that.

Before she knew what was happening, she was seized in a tremendous bear hug that lifted her off her feet. Hiroshi's strong arms wrapped around her, and his beard scratched her cheek. "Thank the *heavens* you are here!" he cried. "I thought for sure we'd lost you. I would never have forgiven myself. Are you all right?" He let Brieze go and her feet returned to the deck. Hiroshi's lips were blue, and the sheen of sweat on his face had turned to frost.

"I'm fine," Brieze sputtered. "Thank you. The pirate ship! Where is it?"

"No sign of 'em," Hiroshi said with a grin. "Let's hope the wind dashed them against the Teeth, or they capsized. Either way I doubt they'll bother us now. We're almost through. Who ever thought being hit by a windspout could be a good thing?"

Brieze hugged herself and shivered. "It's so cold!"

"Ha!" Hiroshi said, clapping her on the shoulder. "That spout took us higher than ships should go. We're right among the peaks. But the thin air won't keep us up here long. We'll sink down to thicker, warmer air soon. Hold fast my little Nagmor slayer." He tousled her hair and then was off, shouting orders.

Brieze looked up. They *were* right among the peaks. Just a few hundred feet above, the Teeth tapered to sharp points against the sky. But already the Teeth seemed to be rising upward as the *Kinzou* drifted downward. That was good, she knew, because they wouldn't have been able to survive long in that life-leaching cold and oxygen-poor air. Some reckless and adventurous airmen had attempted to cross the Teeth by flying over them, but none had ever succeeded.

A short time later, the *Kinzou* settled to a comfortable cruising altitude. An hour later, they passed through the last of the Teeth into open sky. It was the most beautiful shade of lavender she'd ever seen, Brieze thought. The sky was dotted with plump, white, and somehow friendly-seeming cumulus clouds. The crewmen cheered. Below them, the silver-gray surface clouds of Etherium stretched in an unbroken plane to the eastern horizon. Right on the horizon before them, at the very edge of their vision, sat dark smudges that she thought were clouds, but the men recognized as the first glimpse of home—the westernmost mountains of the Eastern Kingdoms. When the lookout called the sighting, the men cheered even louder.

"Ha!" Hiroshi said, giddy with relief. "We're through the

Teeth at last! Suffered nothing more than trading a few shots with pirates and getting knocked about a bit. Didn't lose a man! Many have fared worse. Now there's nothing but fat lazy clouds and familiar currents between us and home."

Brieze turned sternward for a parting gaze at the Wind's Teeth. In the low evening light they looked serene and beautiful, scintillating alluringly, as if there were no dangers hidden in their depths. She realized that the entire time she'd been there, she hadn't taken any notes, made a single close observation or sketch, or done anything else a wizard's apprentice would normally do when presented with the opportunity to study such a geologic marvel. She would have loved to take a sample of those crystals somehow and bring them back to show her father. She would have kept a shiny chunk on her desk as a reminder of her adventure.

"I'll stop back there one day soon," she said softly. She was still in the habit of talking to herself. "Maybe on my way home."

EIGHT

A day out from the Teeth they met a convoy of military airships from the Eastern Kingdoms. There were three large ships, well-armed, and they were heading west. The *Kinzou* and the convoy maneuvered to within easy shouting—and tossing—distance of each other so they could exchange news and mail.

The second-in-command aboard the *Kinzou*, a loud man named Riku who had dragon tattoos snaking up his thickly muscled arms, made the rounds with a canvas mail bag. "Mail for the west!" he shouted. "Western bound mail. Hurry!" Many crewmen, more than Brieze would have expected, pulled letters from inner pockets and tossed them into the sack. Many of them pulled out unsealed letters and hastily scrawled a few last notes before sealing them up and sending them on their way.

Brieze had three letters in an inner pocket of her cloak—the ones she had written Tak, her mother, and her wizard father to keep herself from going crazy. But she'd made the inexperienced traveler's mistake of sealing them up immediately after she'd written them. She wished she could scrawl a few more lines to tell them about everything that had happened since! But there was no time. She would have to write again once she reached Kyo. Riku stood before her. He bowed to her as he held the sack open. "Mail for the west?" he asked politely.

Brieze dropped in the letters to her mother and the wizard. But she hesitated to drop Tak's letter into the sack. She was trying to remember exactly what she'd said to him in her long crazed ramblings. She knew she said a lot of things she never normally would have said. Embarrassing things. Things she would regret later. But to send a letter to her mother and wizard father and not one to Tak would be heartless. He would be crushed.

To stall for time, she asked Riku a question. "Why are so many of the crew sending letters west? Surely they can't have families there."

He reddened and gave her an awkward smile. She'd unthinkingly asked the question in the Western tongue, and he struggled to reply in kind. "Not family. They have…what is word?…sweethearts. Girlfriend."

"Ahhhhh," Brieze said, understanding. "They've got one in every port probably, huh?"

Just like Kaishou Fujiwara, she thought.

Riku lowered his eyes and mumbled something inaudible. Brieze realized he was in a hurry to gather all the mail, but that, for her, he would stand there with the sack open all day if he had to. He would never dare tell her to hurry up and make up her mind.

She dropped Tak's letter into the bag. Riku bowed and

hurried away.

"I'll have to deal with the consequences of *that* later," she said to herself.

As the ships came within tossing distance, mail bags were hurled and caught on both sides. Men leaned over railings and climbed up into rigging to shout news to each other. This was done in a completely haphazard and disorganized fashion. Men everywhere were talking fast and loud in the eastern tongue, and Brieze could only catch a few words and phrases here and there. The men of the *Kinzou* were relating news about their brush with pirates in the Teeth, and also about their encounter with the Nagmor and the Nagmor slayer. Many of them pointed to Brieze. She stood against a rail, and she waved awkwardly at the men from the military ships as they stared at her.

But Brieze soon realized the military men had news just as exciting to relate. She caught the word *ryuujin*, dragonlord, shouted many times, and saw the effect it had on the men of the *Kinzou.* Long after the ships had passed, the men of the *Kinzou* huddled together and talked with tense faces, and the word *ryuujin* came up again and again.

"What's going on?" she asked Hiroshi when he had a moment. "What's the news from the east?"

"Do you know of the rogue wizard we call the Dragonlord, who inhabits the Burning Mountains in the north of our country?" asked Hiroshi.

"Yes, my father warned me to steer completely clear of him. He said the pirates sell him slaves."

"That is true, and it is well you were warned," Hiroshi

said. "It would appear the *ryuujin* is up to something, although exactly what is not clear. His red and golden dragons have been seen flying in groups of twos and threes over many of our mountains, as if scouting or spying, and our ships have encountered them in other lands as well. The Emperor has put the military and the fleet on full alert. He ordered that convoy we passed to make the voyage west to warn your king and our other western allies."

"That was kind of him."

"That may be. But I'm afraid you might not find our country as warm and welcoming to strangers as we would be under normal circumstances."

"I'll manage," Brieze said. As far as she was concerned, if the easterners were distracted by other things, so much the better for her. It might allow her to take care of her business more easily.

* * *

Brieze devoted her last weeks aboard the *Kinzou* to learning as much as she possibly could, not just about the ship and its crew, but about their homeland, language, and culture. She asked the crewmen countless questions, and she spoke to them only in the eastern tongue, so she could get the practice. The men were delighted to answer her questions. They tried to outdo each other in giving her thorough explanations. The one thing they never did, though, was correct her when she made a mistake in the eastern tongue—and she made a lot of them. She had no way of knowing this, so she believed she was making great progress in her fluency.

More than anything else, she loved learning their songs. When they lit their colored lanterns and gathered on the main deck to sing at night, she was irresistibly drawn to them. She sat at the edge of the group and listened. She closed her eyes, memorizing the words and the melodies, whose strange dips and lilts didn't sound as odd to her ears anymore. Soon, she began mouthing the words and singing under her breath. One of her favorite songs was a slow tune about longing for home, sad and sweet at the same time. In the western language, the words went like this:

> *In the land where the rising sun*
> *Kisses the heads of the mountains*
> *In the land where apple and cherry blossoms*
> *Fall like snow in the spring*
> *In the land where my loved one's eyes*
> *Search the sky at evening time*
> *Hoping to see my ship's sail*
>
> *There my heart lies, there my breath sighs*
> *Currents be kind, and weather be fine*
> *And bring me back to my one true home*

One night, as the men sang this song, Brieze joined in. She hadn't meant to, it just happened. One minute she was singing under her breath and the next her voice leapt loud and clear from her mouth. Something moved her to join her voice with the others, and it was thrilling! The song poured out of her, and for a moment she felt the intense pleasure of *belonging*, of expressing the deep emotions they all shared. Goosebumps prickled all along her arms. She smiled broadly, eyes shining, as she sang.

And, one by one, the men's voices dropped out.

Soon, she was singing by herself, until her voice faltered into awkward silence.

The men stared down at their feet. None of them would meet her eyes.

She jumped up, flustered. "I'm sorry…" she stammered. "Did I do something wrong?"

They gave each other uneasy glances. Riku finally cleared his throat and, still not daring to look at her, said, "Please…you sing. We listen."

Brieze turned and fled, mortified. She scrambled down a hatch, bolted along a corridor, and hid herself in the captain's cabin, slamming the door behind her. She flung herself on the narrow bed, punched the pillow a few times, and buried her face in it. From above, she heard the sound of men arguing on the deck. Hiroshi's voice rose above the others, questioning. They answered in plaintive tones.

Soon, Hiroshi knocked at the door of the cabin. "May I come in?"

"Fine," Brieze huffed.

He sat stiffly on the edge of the bed. She kept her face buried in the pillow.

"You did nothing wrong," he said. "It's just that my men have such great deference for you, none would dare raise his voice above yours."

"I only wanted to sing with them. Was that so wrong?"

"No, but you took them by surprise. They didn't know what to do. Please, come join us now. We will all sing together if that is your wish."

"Forget it," she turned on her side to face the wall, hugging the pillow. "It's ruined now."

He sighed. "My men feel badly. They didn't mean to hurt your feelings. They only stopped singing out of respect."

"Respect!" Brieze spat the word as she kicked the wall. "That's all I ever get, and I'm *sick* of it."

Hiroshi fidgeted. He had no experience dealing with the hurt feelings of teenage girls, especially not ones who happened to be wizard's apprentices. He decided that he'd done his best and it was time to beat a delicate retreat. "Tomorrow," he said, closing the cabin door behind him, "this will be a storm that has passed."

Brieze stayed shut in the cabin for the rest of the night, tossing and turning on the bed. She missed her mother, her father, and especially Tak. He was one of the few people who didn't keep his distance from her. He hadn't known who she was when they first met, and he'd been rude, obnoxious, even hostile. She didn't blame him. She'd shot two arrows into his precious airship, after all, as he was trying to sneak onto the floating island. But his rudeness was refreshing. Exciting even. And then, they were thrown together into so many adventures so fast there was no time for distance to develop. They became fast friends. He treated her like an equal.

She missed his quick smile and his dumb jokes. She even missed his swagger and cockiness, just a little, though she wouldn't admit this to anyone but herself. She missed his strong hands and the way they were drawn unabashedly to hers. She missed his kisses…

Ach, his kisses. Best not to think of those now.

She wished his arms were around her. She wondered where he was, what he was doing, and when she would see him again.

NINE

Tak's unit of cadets gathered in their bunkroom after a day of drilling. They had a half hour of free time before evening mess. This was usually a loud, rowdy half hour as the cadets took full advantage of the lack of supervision and blew off steam. The long room with its orderly rows of cots and trunks along each wall was usually filled with whoops and shouts, good natured and not-so-good natured insults flying back and forth, and the occasional spontaneous wrestling—or shoving— match. Even the boys who were tired and wanted nothing more than a short rest before dinner managed to do this loudly, with an excess of stretching and groaning and complaining about the drill sergeant.

But not today. Today was mail day.

Every cadet found a packet of letters on his cot. And so, with pleased murmurs and grunts, they ripped open their letters and stretched out on their cots to read.

Tak found three letters on his cot. One from his mother. Another from his uncle Julius and cousins on Silkmont. And a third from his good friend Luff, a goat herder who lived on Gatmont. He opened and scanned his mother's letter first, just to make sure there was no bad news about his father. Taktinius Spinner senior had been seriously ill since the siege of Selestria. But the letter assured him his father was still on the mend. So he put that letter aside and opened the one from Luff. He grinned as he read, because Luff liked nothing better than to poke fun at Tak for what he called his "fancy-pants, city-boy ways." He did this by mockingly imitating the courtly language used in Selestria.

> *My Dearest and Most Esteemed Taktinius Spinner Junior,*
> *This missive is to inform you that in one month's time I shall be journeying to the city of Selestria with my father, on business of a hircine nature. I most humbly request an audience with you, in order to give your eminence an opportunity to redeem himself after the tremendous and most shameful spanking he received when last we raced our respective airships. I shall call upon you at the academy at my earliest convenience.*
> *Your Most Obedient and Respectful Servant,*
> *Lufftik Herder of Gatmont*

Underneath his signature, in crude lines, Luff had sketched what looked like a Herder family crest, even though the Herders had no official crest. On the background of an oval shield, two goats were doing something rather vulgar, above the family motto, "Watch Where You Step."

Tak's laughter was cut short by the cadet on the bunk next to him. He tossed a letter onto Tak's lap. "This was in my packet by mistake," he said. "It's for you."

It was from Brieze!

It was addressed in her handwriting and sealed with a blob of red wax imprinted with the wizard's seal.

Tak's heart thumped. He tore the letter open. He read no more than a few lines, though, when he double-checked the seal just to make sure the letter truly *was* from Brieze. Yes, that was her seal. This was her handwriting, sort of. But the letter was unlike anything she'd ever written—or anything Tak suspected she was capable of writing. It read like it came from a completely different person. Her other letters to him had always been formal, perfectly composed, with meticulous penmanship. This letter was all over the place, and the writing was downright sloppy in places. Tak's jaw dropped as he read…

> *My Dearest Tak,*
>
> *I've been alone out here for forever now, and I would give anything for you to be here. I was an idiot not to let you come with me. I miss you more than I can say. It's more than an emotion, it feels like a hunger, a craving, a physical need, deep inside of me that only you could satisfy. If you were here with me right now, I would wrap my arms around you and never let go. I would cover you with kisses, from the top of your head down to your toes…*

Tak's slack jaw widened into a dumbfounded, brainless, ear-to-ear grin. The letter went on like that for two pages, describing in detail what she would like to do if he were there and the things she planned to do when they were together again. She used a lot of big words he didn't know, like *tempestuous* and *delectable* and *palpitations*, but he got the general idea.

And then the letter's closing hit him like a frenzy of grekks.

> *Stay warm this winter with thoughts of me…*
> *Love,*
> *B*

Tak gasped.

Love?!

She said *love*.

She never said *love* before.

Clearly, she was unhinged. The loneliness of the journey had gotten to her, scrambled her wits. That was not good. You needed your wits on a voyage like that. She could be a danger to herself. But here was a key question. Had her loneliness prodded her to confess something she truly felt, or had she used the word *love* only because she was so desolate, and unbalanced, and not thinking clearly? Arrrgh! It was just like her to say *love* from half a world away, when he couldn't say anything back or ask any questions.

He read the letter again from start to finish, his heart thumping in his chest. Then he lay back on his cot and let the pages rest on top of his face. He closed his eyes and inhaled deeply, as if he could breathe in her words, and he imagined he caught the faintest scent of her lingering on the paper. A scent like sun-warmed skin and wind through pines in springtime. He murmured some of her words and phrases. Then he sat up and read the letter again, savoring it slowly. But it was over too soon, so he read it just one more time.

By the time it occurred to him to look up and see what time it was, the bunkroom was empty. Everyone else had gone to mess. He was late! Hastily he jumped up, stashed the letter in a pocket, and dashed off to join his comrades for dinner. If he moved fast, he might get there before anyone noticed he was late and gave him a demerit.

✳   ✳   ✳

Like most rooms built by sky riders, the academy mess hall was made to let in as much of the sky as possible. The ceiling was high—sky riders hated to be crowded by low ceilings—and inset with glass skylights. The windows were wide and tall, and even though it was winter they were open a crack, letting in a hint of the chill mountain air and the rosy light of the sinking sun. The rows of tables were crowded with cadets eating and talking fast. The hubbub of hundreds of conversations echoed off the walls. The noise seemed even livelier and more intense than usual. The room was buzzing. Excitement crackled in the air.

Tak grabbed a plate of chow from the kitchen in the back and found a seat at his unit's table. As soon as he plunked his plate and mug down on the pine planks, one of them asked him, "Did you hear the news? Did she tell you?"

"Did who tell me?"

"Your girlfriend. In her letter. Did she tell you what she did?"

"How do you know I got a letter from Brieze?"

"Oh come on! You sat there reading it over and over, mooning over it and sniffing it like a scented hankie. Who else could it be from? Your mother?" There was a general chuckle at that.

"So did she tell you?" another pressed him. "What did she say about it?"

"About what?" Tak asked, flummoxed by everyone's expectant stares.

"He doesn't know," one said.

"Know what?" Tak asked.

The cadet across from him took a deep breath and announced, "Your girlfriend killed a Nagmor!"

"And nearly wrecked flying through the Wind's Teeth!" another said.

"And got attacked by pirates!" a third chimed in.

"But mostly…*she killed a Nagmor*!" The one across from him said. "She saved an Eastern merchant ship and its crew."

Tak sat there and gaped, his food and drink forgotten. The information he was getting from his fellow cadets was so at odds with Brieze's letter that his mind couldn't make sense of it. His brain stalled out. There was nothing but luff and chatter between his ears.

So they explained it all to him. A delegate of Eastern ships from Kyo had arrived at castle Selestria yesterday, bringing much news, including news about Brieze. She was traveling to Kyo on a ship called the *Kinzou*. She'd saved the ship from a Nagmor attack, killing the beast with some kind of explosive device. In later versions of the story, she blew the Nagmor to bits using only the power of her mind. Such was the opinion of wizards in general and Brieze in particular. But the current version stuck more or less to the truth. The news had raced like the wind all over Selemont, all the way to the academy on Larkspur. No one in the history of the Kingdom of Spire had ever killed a Nagmor before. It was sensational!

The Eastern delegation brought more news. The *Kinzou* had passed through the Wind's Teeth, nearly wrecking there and trading cannon fire with pirates to boot. And what was more, the whole reason the Easterners had come to Selemont in the first place was to warn the King that the Dragonlord of the East was up to something. His red and gold dragons were being sighted everywhere. The Eastern navy was on high alert. The King was expected to put the Western fleet on high alert too, especially since the *Dragonbane* had never arrived for its diplomatic mission to the Kingdom of Frost. The ship and all her crew—including Admiral Adamus Strake— were missing and presumed lost, perhaps due to foul play by the Dragonlord.

"The Eastern ships must have brought Brieze's letter," the cadet on Tak's right said. "She didn't mention any of this?"

Tak fiddled with the food on his plate. "Nope."

"Well, what *did* she say?"

Tak dropped his fork with a disgusted sigh. "Apparently

nothing."

There was an awkward silence around the table.

"Well…maybe she didn't want you to worry, you know?" someone offered.

Tak had no way of knowing that Brieze's letter had been written before her adventures. That she'd made the mistake of sealing it immediately and had no way to scrawl even a hint of her latest news before the mail bag came around on the *Kinzou*. He stood up abruptly. Grabbed up his plate and mug. "I've got to go."

As he dropped his plate and mug off at the kitchen, he caught the eye of Jon Cutter junior, the skinny giant. The boy was sitting at a table in the back with the other lumber-jacks. Tak nodded to Jon but the Cutter boy only stared back at him. His eyes narrowed, studying Tak intensely. He chewed slowly and deliberately as if, even when eating, his jaw was disinclined to move.

Tak stalked out of the mess hall, aware of all the eyes on him and the whispered conversations starting up behind his back. He made up his mind. He was going to Kyo. He was-n't going to formally request leave or a postponement of his studies. He was going to leave a letter for the academy presi-dent that night, and take off under the cover of darkness. That would have to do.

Brieze was half a world away, and in danger. Already she'd been threatened by Nagmor and pirates. And now this business with the Dragonlord. He needed to be at her side. He should have insisted on going with her right from the start. And she'd practically invited him to come in her letter.

Right?

When he found her, she would have some explaining to do.

Especially about this word *love*.

* * *

With a parachute pack strapped securely to his back, and a heavy duffel bag crammed with clothes and gear over his shoulder, Tak snuck out onto the academy dock where private ships were moored. The *Arrow* was there, down near the end of the dock, bobbing on the wind and, as ever, tugging eagerly at its mooring ropes. It was dark, with a sliver of moon high up in the cloudy sky. The dock was not guarded. Still, Tak crept along as quietly as he could. He would have a hard time explaining his presence there to anyone who noticed and challenged him. It was well past lights out, and he should have been snoring in his cot in the bunkroom with the other cadets.

A light snow dusted the dock. A strong winter wind nudged the moored ships about. The wooden clunks they made as they bobbed and bumped against the dock, the slap of ropes against masts, the flapping of sails, covered the creak of Tak's footsteps. With agility that came from long practice and familiarity, he hopped off the dock into the *Arrow* without making it list or rock. He set down his duffel bag on the thwart bench and undid the rear mooring line, casting it off. He quickly did the same with the front mooring line, casting the rope toward the dock.

Somebody caught the rope.

Tak yelped. A figure stood on the dock with the rope in one hand.

A tall, skinny figure. Nearly seven feet tall, to be exact. Moonlight glimmered in his wild, curly red hair. His eyes gleamed in the dark.

"Jon!" Tak said. "What are you doing here?"

From their last conversation, Tak gathered that Jon was a man of few words. But Tak didn't know Jon had been un-usually talkative then. He rarely bothered to use words when a look or gesture would do. His eyes and his face could be eloquent. At the moment, he was giving Tak a look that said, clearly as any words, *I'm going with you.*

Tak fumbled for a lie. "I'm not going anywhere…," he stammered. "I'm just going out for a midnight ride. To clear my head. I'll be back in an hour or two."

Jon sighed and shook his head to convey that he disliked being lied to. His eyes went knowingly to Tak's overstuffed duffel bag, sitting in plain sight on the bench, then locked with Tak's eyes. *Nice try.*

Jon wore a traveling cloak over his workmen's clothes. A standard sky rider pack was strapped to his back: parachute compartment above, backpack below. He also carried a heavy duffel bag slung over one shoulder. And the hand that wasn't holding the mooring rope gripped a tall, double-bladed axe, nearly as tall as Jon was himself.

"Why?" Tak asked.

Jon thought about his answer for a while, and finally had to use words. He cleared his throat. "You shouldn't go alone. I think my dad would want me to go with you."

Tak closed his eyes and considered. A voyage across the Eastern Emptiness was a daunting, lonely thing. He knew this from airmen's stories, but Brieze's letter made it powerfully clear. If she, who was naturally so reserved and self-reliant, who seemed to *need* her solitude, had been reduced to an emotional mess, Tak could only imagine what the journey would do to *him*. And he had to admit he'd feel safer traveling with Jon. There'd be dangers out there, and Jon had proved he had Tak's back and could handle himself in a fight.

Tak opened his eyes. "All right," he said. "Get in."

Jon dropped the mooring rope, tossed his duffel bag into the *Arrow*, and jumped ungracefully in after it. The *Arrow* listed sharply, then rocked as Jon scrambled for balance, using his axe to steady himself. Tak frowned. The Cutters of Pinemont flew in airships like everybody else, but they also lived *closer to the ground*, as people often said of them. They didn't have an instinct for the finer points of flying. They spent much of their time in forests, with their feet planted in the dirt, hacking at trees. They walked ridiculously long distances, distances that other sky riders would travel only by airship. Walking was considered an unsophisticated and undignified mode of transportation by most sky riders, especially those on Selemont.

Jon shoved them off from the dock with the handle of his axe. Tak pushed on the tiller until the bow came around into the wind. He raised and angled the *Arrow's* sail, then tightened the lines as the sail bellied full of wind and the ship lifted and glided out into the dark.

Despite Jon's clumsiness, Tak's heart was lighter knowing he'd have company for the journey. He couldn't help grinning. "It's gonna be a long voyage," he said. "Know any good songs or stories to pass the time?"

Jon chewed the patchy beard under his lower lip, cleared his throat with a little growl, and spit over the side. "Don't know any songs. Don't like stories," he said.

"Well, what *do* you like?"

"Quiet, mostly." Jon pulled his cloak tighter around himself and settled into his seat.

Tak contemplated that for a while.

"Well," he finally said with a sigh. "We've got to go see my parents before we get underway. Will you be polite and talk to *them*?"

Jon nodded an affirmative.

TEN

Tak's father, Taktinius Spinner senior, sat at the head of the polished oak table in the Spinner's kitchen, glowering. His shaggy, silver-streaked black hair was mussed with sleep. His eyes blinked blearily. His usually neatly trimmed black beard had grown bushy and unkempt. The collar of his nightshirt hung open, exposing the little hollow at his throat, just above the collarbone on the right side. An artery pulsed there whenever he was upset. It started pulsing the moment Tak's loud knocking at the back door had roused him from sleep, and it was throbbing wildly now that Tak had explained his reason for coming and his plan to travel east.

"Unacceptable!" Tak senior pounded the tabletop with a fist. "Utter foolishness!"

Tak's mother, Marghorettia Spinner, had ladled out bowls of her famous egg soup for everyone from the pot simmering above the hearth fire. At the thumping of Tak senior's fist, everyone's soup trembled and rippled in the wooden bowls. Jon, who'd been staring straight down into his bowl, shoveling the soup in methodically with a spoon, paused and looked up.

Tak was about to respond when his father fell into a coughing fit—a long, lingering one. The wet, raspy, drawn-out coughs made Tak's throat ache in sympathy. Marghorettia got up from her chair and handed her husband a handkerchief, and then rubbed his back. Tak studied his father's face more closely in the firelight and noticed his shrunken cheeks, the dark, puffy circles under his eyes. Beads of sweat glistened on his forehead.

Taktinius Spinner senior had been sick ever since the siege of Selestria. He'd been badly wounded in the leg, and he'd been taken by a fever that none of the physicians in the city of Selestria could do anything to stop. He'd tossed and turned and sweated in his bed, delirious, with Tak and Marghorettia at his side. The hastily stitched up wound in his thigh turned a swollen, angry red. Streaks of red spread from the festering wound up and down the skin of his leg. The physicians told Tak and his mother to prepare for the worst. Many of those wounded in the siege had already died from the wound fever, as it was called.

Once again, the wizard saved the day. As always, he had an outlandish theory. He said that a battle was raging inside of Tak senior's body. Tiny invisible animals called "germs"—so small they could not be seen—had entered his body through the wound in his leg. The germs were attacking, and the fever was the body's way of trying to fight them off. He rendered Tak senior unconscious by holding a rag soaked with a strange-smelling substance over his nose. He cut open the stitches and cleaned out the wound, then stitched it carefully back up. He gave Marghorettia a gallon-sized bottle of a greenish medicine that he said would kill the germs. She was to administer one spoonful three times a day. The medicine worked. The fever broke after a week, and in another week Tak senior was able to rise from bed and limp around, with the aid of a cane. He was growing a little stronger every day.

"My dear," Marghorettia said, rubbing her husband's back. "Did you take your medicine today?"

"I don't need that stuff anymore," he said. "I've been taking it for weeks, and I'm feeling better."

"The wizard said three spoonfuls a day until the bottle is empty, even if you feel better."

"The stuff tastes like goat piss," he growled. "And who ever heard of tiny invisible animals? It's nonsense."

"That nonsense saved your life, and you will take your medicine."

The look on her face prevented any further argument. She fetched the bottle and administered three spoonfuls of the medicine to Tak senior, who grumbled and winced as he swallowed each one. The large bottle was still half full. Clearly, there would be much more of the awful-tasting stuff to swallow in the weeks to come.

When his father's grumbling had settled into silence, Tak ventured, "You voyaged to the Eastern Kingdoms once father. You said it was the best trip of your life."

"That was different. I was part of a convoy. We were on a trading mission."

"But Brieze is in danger. She needs my help."

Tak senior raised an eyebrow. "In danger from what?"

"Nagmor. Pirates. And now maybe the Dragonlord."

"Those are just rumors. And in any case, that girl can more than take care of herself. She doesn't need any boyfriend rushing in like a fool to rescue her. She'd probably end up having to save *you*. She killed that Nagmor all by herself, if you believe the accounts."

Tak's mother chimed in. "Brieze very clearly said she didn't want you to go with her. Won't she be angry if you show up? You know how she gets."

"I just got a letter from her. She kind of asked me to come."

His mother narrowed her eyes skeptically. "Kind of?"

"She said she misses me and wishes I was there. She said she wished she'd invited me."

"That's not exactly an invitation."

"Coming from Brieze, it's close enough. How can I stay here doing dumb drills at the academy when she's all alone over there and in danger?"

Tak senior pulled at this hair in exasperation. Tufts of it stuck out from his head at odd angles. "Dumb drills? All your life you've dreamed of the academy, and now that you're there you want to quit already!"

Tak shrugged. "Things changed for me after the siege. I don't know what I want anymore."

"Exactly!" Tak senior pounded the table again. "You've hit on the crux of the issue. This isn't about Brieze, it's about what *you* are going to do with *your* life. I always wanted you to go into the family business, but I never forced you. I was proud when the king granted you entrance to the academy.

And now you want to throw that away and make our family look foolish, for what? To go gallivanting and adventuring on the other side of the world? To spend time with your girlfriend? What are you going to do when you return? What profession will you enter? You need to get your head out of the clouds and get serious about your life."

"Fine father," Tak huffed. "I promise I will, when I return." He didn't try to hide his irritation. His father's words struck a nerve, a raw one. On some level, Tak knew his father was right. And this rankled him. His face reddened.

Tak's disrespectful tone fanned the flames of his father's anger. "No!" he said, standing up so abruptly that his chair toppled backward. He leaned on the table with trembling arms. "You won't do it when you return, because you're not going. Your mother and I have been too lenient on you for too long. We've spoiled you. You will get serious about your life now!"

The word *spoiled* set Tak off. He hated it when people called him that. He stood up too, pushing his char back, and glowered at his father. "I *am* going," he said with a clenched jaw. "Just try to stop me."

"Tak…" Marghorettia gasped. Her son had never spoken to his father this way before.

Jon, his soup forgotten, stared at the two men as they locked eyes over the table. He was reminded of two rams, heads down and horns pointed at each other, about to charge.

For just a moment when Tak spoke so defiantly, Tak senior had looked shocked and dismayed. Then the anger washed over him, redoubled. If Tak had been a few years younger, he would have just grabbed his son by the scruff of the neck and forced him upstairs to his room. But his son was no longer a child. He was a young man. A strong and determined one. He'd fought in the siege of Selestria. Tak senior knew that in his weakened state he was no match physically for his son. He couldn't stop him by force. And that made him furious. He had only one card left to play, and he played it.

"If you quit the academy," he said, his voice full of venom. "If you anger the king and give people reason to laugh at us Spinners and talk behind our backs, as you have done all your life, I promise you this, there will be no place in this house for you when you return. You will be entirely on your own."

Marghorettia gasped again. "Now just settle down," she said. "Both of you. You're not being reason—"

"Fine with me, *father*," Tak sneered. At that moment, he *hated* his father. Deep down, those words hurt him more than any words ever had. "As you wish," he spat. He turned his back and stalked out of the kitchen.

"You'll be sorry!" Tak senior called after him, then fell into another coughing fit, longer and more violent than the first. His face reddened and he struggled to catch his breath. Marghorettia had been about to chase after her son, but she attended to her husband instead. She righted his chair and helped him sit down in it. She brought him a glass of water. She rubbed his back as the fit subsided.

Jon used the distraction to slip out of the kitchen after

Tak. But not before picking up his bowl with both hands and draining it in one long gulp. He wiped his lips with his sleeve and grunted with satisfaction. The soup was that good.

* * *

Like most buildings in the city of Selestria, Ouranos Outfitters was built directly into the steep side of the mountain. The sprawling, three-story shop was fashioned from pine timber and blocks of mountain stone. It sat in the southeastern quadrant of the city, at the intersection of the Southeast Winding Way and the third turn of the Western Spiral Road. And as with all buildings constructed by sky riders, the main entrance was at the top story, not the bottom. A wide wooden dock projected from the third story, jutting out over the street below.

It was well past midnight when Tak and Jon tied the *Arrow* up at this dock. It was deserted, but the shop was open, as Tak knew it would be. The two lamps flanking the front door were lit, illuminating the sign that hung above it.

Ouranos & Sons Outfitters
Open Day & Night
Your Journey Starts Here

A bell chimed as the boys entered. Old man Ouranos himself sat on the high stool behind the counter, reading by candlelight. The older he got, the less he was able to sleep, so he usually took the night shift, then napped in the back while his sons ran the place during the day. His eyebrows shot up when he saw the Chief Sailspinner's son in his shop at that hour. The boy had a reputation in the city. He had a knack for getting himself in trouble. He'd been hauled before the authorities on various charges more times than Ouranos could remember. But more recently, he'd fought in the siege of Selestria and received a medal of valor and a special commendation from the King himself.

What was the boy up to now?

Ouranos set aside his book and put on his best smile. The Spinners were good customers. And they made the best spider-silk sails in the kingdom. Sails that were sold in that very shop, and sold very well, at a nice profit.

"Young Taktinius, so nice to see you again. To what do I owe the pleasure?"

His voice echoed in the enormous room, a room that took up the entire top story of the building. The ceiling hovered twenty feet above their heads. And on every wall, from floor to ceiling, there were shelves. Every possible thing a traveler could need or want for an airship voyage could be found on those shelves. The place smelled of freshly cut lumber and freshly oiled tackle, of new rope and pine pitch. To Tak, who'd first visited the shop as a small boy riding on his father's shoulders, the place always smelled like adventure.

Tak leaned on the counter. Jon stood behind him, gaping up at the stacks and stacks of shelves. They didn't have shops like this on Pinemont.

"I need a few things," Tak said, trying to sound casual. "For a trip I'm taking."

"I see. A trip where?"

Tak hesitated. But he needed to tell Ouranos the truth. That way, the shopkeeper could make sure to supply him with everything he needed. "The Eastern Kingdoms," he said. "The city of Kyo to be exact."

The old man's eyebrows shot up again. "Now? In winter?"

"Now," Tak said.

"Do your parents know about this little trip you're taking?"

"They do," Tak said, meeting the old man's eyes to show he was telling the truth. Some of it, anyway.

"Very well."

It took an hour for them to gather everything that was needed and to load it onto the *Arrow*. Old man Ouranos scurried up and down ladders and hauled things off shelves. A lifetime of that kind of work made him strong and nimble. The *Arrow's* cargo compartments were small—the ship was built for speed, not for long voyages. But they managed to get everything stowed or securely tied down. Tak frowned as he saw all the stuff accumulating on his ship. Packages of ship's biscuit wrapped in waterproof oilcloth. Sacks of dried beans and goat jerky. Cask after cask of water. The supplies were heavy. They would slow the *Arrow* down, add extra time to the voyage.

They would also be expensive.

Ouranos senior tallied everything up on a slip of paper.

He wrote the total cost at the bottom.

It was a big number.

He cleared his throat and asked delicately, "And how will you be paying for this today, young sir?" He looked at Tak as if he hoped the boy would reach into his pockets and pull out fistfuls of coins. Tak had some money. But not nearly enough. And he would need what he had for when he reached Kyo.

Tak fiddled with the ring on his left hand. It was a silver signet ring. Its flat head was engraved with a triangle composed of three curving lines, representing a sail in the wind.

"Shall I put this on the Spinner family's line of credit, which is excellent and always good here?" Ouranos asked, though without enthusiasm. He strongly preferred cash up front.

"No," Tak said, removing the ring and handing it to him. "Take this."

The old man gasped. Jon's eyes widened, and he looked at Tak. *Are you crazy?*

That ring was the Spinner family ring.

For the well-to-do families in the Kingdom of Spire, family rings were extremely important. They were worth much more than the gold or silver they were made of. They were beyond price. Handing over one's ring was a symbol of defeat or surrender. There were stories of men who had refused to trade their rings for their lives.

It was not the sort of thing you traded for dried beans and goat jerky.

"I can't accept that…." Ouranos sputtered.

"I don't have anything else," Tak said.

Ouranos pulled at the white hairs on his chin and considered. He was a shrewd man. He knew Taktinius senior would be beyond furious if he learned that Ouranos Outfitters had accepted a Spinner family ring as payment. That would be extremely bad for business. On the other hand, Tak senior wasn't getting any younger, and he was rumored to be in questionable health. It was entirely possible the boy might one day be Chief Sailspinner. One day soon. How to negotiate this deal and stay on both their good sides?

"I tell you what," he said. "I will not accept the ring as payment, but I will hold onto it temporarily as collateral *in lieu* of payment, until such time as payment can be made."

"That is acceptable to me," Tak said.

Jon whistled with surprise. The audacity of the moment loosened his tongue. "Wow," he said. "I thought your dad was mad *before*."

ELEVEN

The *Kinzou* reached the mountains of the Eastern King-doms just as the first real snow of winter fell. Fat, wet flakes whirled thickly in the sky. They clung to every rope and line of the ship, outlining them in white. To Brieze, it looked very pretty.

The *Kinzou* flew northeast, keeping the mountains close on their starboard side, making for the city of Kyo at the heart of the Eastern Kingdoms. The crew was in high spirits. Men sang and whistled as they hauled on ropes or scrubbed decks, their breath coming out in cheery puffs. Captain Hiroshi grinned broadly, his thumbs hooked into his belt, and he breathed deeply, savoring the air. Snowflakes decorated his beard. All the tension had gone out of him. He no longer shouted his orders but gave them in a soft voice, as if they were afterthoughts.

Brieze leaned on a rail near the bow, wrapped in a warm cloak, and studied the mountains as they passed.

She'd never seen mountains like these. She had studied maps and pictures, but drawings were nothing like the real thing in front of you. Instead of stretching out in a long, zigzagging chain like the Highspire Mountains, the eastern mountains were grouped tightly together. To Brieze, they looked like *herds* of mountains, as if they had all decided to huddle together. It was stunning to see so much *solidness* all in one place. It was as if the mountains had banded together to challenge the dominance of the sky and vastness of the sea of clouds surrounding them.

The kingdom's four main mountain masses stretched out before her—Ushu on her right, Koku to the northeast, Onshu beyond that, and Kaido off in the northerly distance, nearly lost in the haze. They had once been separate kingdoms, which is why they were still called the Eastern Kingdoms even though they'd been united under one Emperor more than a century ago. The *Kinzou* was making for Onshu, home to the capitol city of Kyo.

The eastern mountains were different in another way. The Highspire Mountains were covered with pines, and from a distance they appeared pleasantly green. The eastern mountains were bare. Their predominant colors were the brown and gray of naked earth and stone. Through her spyglass, Brieze saw the mountains were not completely treeless. She spotted small pines here and there. And there were large, orderly orchards terraced into the mountainsides with rows of apple, cherry, and plum trees. But the branches of these orchard trees were bare and dusted with snow.

Houses clustered into villages on the mountainsides and grew into cities crowning many of the peaks. The roofs of the houses were covered with clay shingles and painted in bright colors, mostly vivid green and blue and yellow. The roofs all curved upward at the corners, so unlike the flat roofs of the west. This strange little architectural quirk made Brieze feel how far she was from home. It reminded her that she was in a strange, unfamiliar land with strange, unfamiliar rules and ways of doing things.

On the third day after they entered the Eastern Kingdoms, they reached the capitol city of Kyo.

Brieze had never imagined a city larger than Selestria, which took up the entire top third of Selemont, Spire's tallest mountain. But the city of Kyo entirely covered not just *one* but *three* mountains. These three mountains were nestled close together, so close that a system of gravity-defying arched stone bridges connected their lower flanks, making the mountains seem to be reaching out and grabbing each other with long, spindly limbs. As the *Kinzou* edged closer to the city, Brieze could see nothing of the original surface of any of the three mountains. They had been completely transformed—carved and crafted into stone walls and towers, pillared houses and paved streets. Even the city's parks and green spaces looked man made. All the roofs were brightly painted and curved upward at the corners. They glittered in the noon sun. Triangular flags and pennants flew from the rooftops, flapping in the crisp, clear winter air.

The port of Kyo was as large as the city of Selestria. It took up the top third of one of Kyo's mountains. A series of stone quays ringed the mountaintop, the smallest ring near the peak, the largest about a half-mile below. It looked as if a stack of circular stone shelves had been built into the mountain, each one completely encircling it. They were supported from below by clever stone buttresses. Rectangular, airship-sized berths had been cut into them, with mooring posts that looked like stone pillars with gigantic iron chains.

Taking in the size and splendor of Kyo, Brieze felt a strange feeling she couldn't quite identify. It was a little like jealousy, and a little like fear. But not really like either of them. She realized the feeling was humility. She was feeling humble. "Interesting," she said to herself. "I haven't felt that in a while."

Captain Hiroshi took the wheel of the *Kinzou* himself and steered it toward one of the rectangular berths. Every man took a position at one rope or line or another. The steering and the sails had to be handled just right. If the ship came in too fast, it would crash into its berth, causing damage. If it came in too slow, it would sink too fast and miss the berth entirely, hitting the mountainside below.

Brieze held her breath during the maneuver, and she didn't let it out until the bow gently kissed the stone quay and the ship came to rest snugly in its berth. The *Devious*, still tied to the bowsprit above the bow, didn't suffer a scratch. The *Kinzou's* mooring chains were hooked on. The crew furled the sails, and the ship went still. Brieze felt the stillness of the deck in the soles of her shoes.

They were home.

The crew cheered loudly, and she cheered with them.

But it wasn't time to celebrate yet. There was still much to do. As eager as they were to return to their homes and families, not a man on the *Kinzou* would rest until their cargo of timber had been unloaded, sold, and turned into hard cash jingling in their purses.

"All right men, you know what to do!" Hiroshi shouted. "I want our cargo unloaded and secured by nightfall!"

The crew got to work.

A squad of uniformed men stood dockside, closely watching the activity aboard the *Kinzou*.

"Who are they?" Brieze asked.

Hiroshi sighed. "That's our navy being on high alert I'm sure," he said. "Come on. I expect they'll want to have a word with you. They'll be questioning all foreigners entering the country now."

Hiroshi led Brieze down a gangplank to the dock. To her surprise, she couldn't walk straight. She staggered and struggled to find her balance. After so much time living on a constantly rocking airship, walking on solid, unmoving ground felt strange. Her body kept wanting to sway back and forth.

Hiroshi laughed and took her arm. "Easy does it, my little Nagmor-slayer. You'll get your land legs back soon."

He greeted the leader of the navy squad good-naturedly and was greeted cordially in return. The squad was dressed much like airmen of the West, with tight-fitting uniforms, high polished boots, and close-cropped hair. But their uniforms were gray, not blue, and the black scabbards of the swords at their sides were inlaid with characters of Eastern writing.

Hiroshi and the squad leader talked too quickly for Brieze to pick out more than a few words. Then the leader asked her a rapid question, and she was surprised to find she didn't understand at all.

"He wants to know who you are, what your business is here, and how long you'll be staying," Hiroshi said in the Western tongue.

She responded to the leader in the Eastern tongue, but his brow furrowed and he looked questioningly at Hiroshi.

"He is having difficulty with your accent," Hiroshi said. "I'll translate."

Brieze was taken aback. None of the crew aboard the *Kinzou* had any trouble with her "accent." But she supposed in a city as large as Kyo there must be many different accents and even dialects.

"Tell him I'm here to visit and learn about Eastern culture. I'll be staying through the spring," she said.

Captain Hiroshi related that to the leader—and much more. From the words she could pick out and his gestures, Brieze understood he was telling the story about their encounter with the Nagmor. The leader's eyes widened with surprise, and the men murmured among themselves. They looked at her with new interest and respect. The leader asked Hiroshi several questions, then explained something in an apologetic tone.

"He needs to know where you'll be lodging," Hiroshi said. "I told him I'll secure a room for you at Mama Kasshoku's boarding house on Little Kyomont—it's a very safe and respectable place, by the way—and that I'll personally escort you there."

This was all coming at Brieze fast. She hadn't really thought about where she'd stay in Kyo. If she had wanted, she could have had her father obtain a letter from the King that would have allowed her to stay at Spire's embassy in Kyo. But she had wanted to enter the city on the down-low, and keep her business to herself.

It didn't seem like that was going to happen.

"That's fine I guess," she huffed.

The squad leader bowed to her and said the Eastern word for "Welcome," enunciating slowly and clearly as if speaking to a child. "*Yo-koso.*"

Brieze scowled, then caught herself and faked a smile. She bowed and said "Thank you" slowly and clearly back, "*Ari-gatou.*"

When the men had gone off, she said, "Did you have to tell him about the Nagmor? I don't feel the need to be a celebrity in this city. I don't want everyone knowing my business."

"You want to meet with the Fujiwaras, right?"

"Well, yes."

"Trust me, this is the best way. Now, let's get your stuff and get you to Mama Kasshoku's. They'll be checking later to make sure you're staying there."

Brieze grabbed some things from the *Devious* and stuffed them into her backpack. Some clothes, including her last set of clean clothes, her combs and pins, a bar of soap, her journals and stationary, ink and quill. She checked her purse. She had a fair number of coins, but she had no idea how long her money would last in Kyo. She hoped Mama Kasshoku's wasn't an expensive place.

She felt sad at leaving the *Kinzou.* It had been her home for more than a month. She would miss it, and its crew. She wanted to say goodbye to them. But the men were all so busy. Already, they were hauling the first of the large pine trunks out of the cargo hold and carrying it across the deck. No one seemed to notice that she was leaving. She sighed, shouldered her backpack, and walked down the gangplank to where Hiroshi waited.

"So where is this Mama Kasshoku's?" she asked, more sulkily than she intended. No one cared she was leaving.

"There," Hiroshi said. He pointed out across the quay at the smallest of Kyo's three mountains, called Little Kyo-mont. It looked to be several miles away. Still, in the crisp, clear winter air, Brieze could make out some of the larger buildings and wider streets. She squinted as if she might be able to pick out Mama Kasshoku's from where they stood.

"Well," she said, "where's our ship? Or do you want to go in the *Devious*?"

Hiroshi laughed. "We can't fly there, my dear."

"Can't fly? Why not?" The airspace around Kyo was thick and swarming with airships. Small ships swooped over their heads as they spoke. It made no sense that they couldn't fly.

"You have much to learn about the city of Kyo," he said. "There are many, *many* people here. If they let everybody fly, the sky would be so crowded the ships would do nothing but crash into each other."

Brieze gestured at the sky. "Well, all *those* people are flying."

"To fly in the city of Kyo, you need a permit, which is expensive and takes time."

"Well how in the heavens are we supposed to get there then?"

Hiroshi grinned. "We walk."

Brieze stared at him as if he'd suggested they hop all the way to Mama Kasshoku's on one foot. "Seriously," she said. "How are we getting there?"

"It's only three miles. A good hour's walk at the most. And it will be a great way for you to see the city and meet some of its people."

Brieze swallowed. Hiroshi was serious. Her heart sank even lower. In the Kingdom of Spire, and especially in the capital city of Selemont, walking was considered an unsophisticated and generally socially unacceptable way of getting around. It was fine for short trips—across the street say, or down to the end of the block. But any more significant excursion required an airship.

Brieze was more of a walker than most Westerners. She'd walked a lot growing up on Footmont, a mountain whose impoverished residents had no choice but to use their feet to travel. On the farm where she grew up, the rickety old airship her grandfather owned was used only infrequently, to transport crops or animals to the market in the big town at Mountainhead. When she became the wizard's apprentice and moved to his island, she took walks there to explore the place. This was considered odd by some. But then, everyone on the wizard's island was odd in some way.

But still—to walk *three miles*? For an *hour*? That was hard for Brieze to wrap her head around. She lifted one of her feet and inspected the thin sole of her shoe. It was not a shoe made for walking. None of her shoes were. Her shoulders slumped. Already, the pack on her back felt heavy.

"I'm going to need a better pair of shoes," she sighed.

Hiroshi took the backpack from her and slung it over his shoulder. "I will carry this for you. But before we go, there is one thing…"

The tone of his voice made Brieze look up from the contemplation of her shoe. Hiroshi was grinning, and his eyes were shining. Suddenly, Riku was kneeling in front of her, holding out what appeared to be a heavy drawstring purse.

"What is this?" she asked. The activity aboard the *Kinzou* had stopped. All the men were gathered on the main deck. They all faced her.

"For the saving of our lives and our cargo, my men decided that you be made an honorary member of the crew," Hiroshi said. "Each has given one piece of silver from his anticipated profits. That's eighty-one pieces of silver, about the standard crewman's share of what we expect to make. We'll adjust it as necessary should profits prove higher."

Brieze's mouth opened and closed. "I can't take it. It's too much."

"Take it!" Hiroshi hissed under his breath. "Otherwise you dishonor them."

Brieze took the purse. It felt as heavy as it looked. She looked up at the crew, grinning at her. Not knowing what else to do, she bowed deeply to them.

As one man, they bowed back.

Someone began to sing. Another man joined him, and then another. Soon they were all singing. Singing loudly in their deep, throaty voices. People walking along the quay stopped and listened. It was her favorite song. The one about returning home to the land of apple and cherry blossoms.

There my heart lies, there my breath sighs
Currents be kind, and weather be fine
And bring me back to my one true home

Brieze blinked rapidly. Her throat tightened.

"Oh crap," she muttered to herself. "I'm going to cry."

She partly fought it, and partly just let it happen. She blinked and let the tears roll down her cheeks. She was grinning and mortified at the same time. Hiroshi discreetly handed her a handkerchief. She dabbed at her cheeks. Her face was flushed and hot.

The song ended. The crew burst into cheers and waves and shouted well-wishes. Brieze waved and shouted back.

"Now we go," Hiroshi said. "Ready?"

She grinned up at him. "Right now, I think I could walk back to the Kingdom of Spire if I had to."

TWELVE

Brieze walked with Captain Hiroshi along the quay, passing warehouses and shipping company offices. Throngs of dockworkers called to each other or sang as they loaded or unloaded cargo. There was a lot of noise. Brieze and the captain descended a wide stone stairway cut into the mountainside and came to the entrance of one of those impossible bridges she had seen from the air. It rose high like an arch, dwindling to a thin ribbon in the distance as it ascended to its peak and then descended toward Little Kyomont.

The bridge was crowded. They joined a line of people going to Little Kyomont on the right hand side. They passed a steady stream of people on the left heading to the port. The wind was stiff—and cold! Brieze huddled behind the protection of Hiroshi's broad back as they walked. Her feet were already starting to ache. Even though her braid was weighed down with a polished stone tied to the end, it whipped about in the heavy wind and nearly smacked a passerby in the face. Brieze grabbed it, pulled it over her shoulder, and held onto it. The view of the city from the bridge's peak was breathtaking, but when she slowed her pace to admire it, someone behind her stepped on her heels and muttered something unfriendly. She picked up her pace.

They stepped off the bridge into the throng of people crowding the streets of Little Kyomont. There were so many bodies that Brieze felt the warmth of them as the churning crowd closed in around her. The voices were like the roar of a waterfall in her ears. She heard shouting and laughter, and the plucky twang of some stringed instrument. She smelled grilling meat and baking bread. Exotic spices. Merchants hawked their wares. Everyone was dressed in bright colors, padded coats of scarlet and emerald and sky-blue embroidered with silver and gold.

Brieze made Hiroshi stop for a moment while she sat on a curb and took off a shoe to remove a pebble that had found its way under her heel. Her foot was clad in a grimy sock she'd been wearing for weeks. There hadn't been many opportunities to change or bathe on the *Kinzou*. She tried to massage the ache out of her foot. "Is this a festival?" she asked Hiroshi, to stall for time. She had to shout to be heard above the crowd.

"No," he said, "Just an ordinary day." He offered her his arm to help her up.

She put the shoe back on. She took his arm reluctantly and groaned as he hauled her to her feet.

They continued walking.

Strangely enough, a part of Brieze relaxed as she shouldered her way through the crowd. It was a part of her that had been tense for so long she'd forgotten it could be any other way. She considered it normal. She relaxed as she realized that every single face in the crowd was just like hers. Growing up on Footmont, her golden skin, her straight black hair, and her dark, almond-shaped eyes instantly set her apart from everyone else. They drew strange looks at the very least, and often worse. As a child, she'd learned to go through life with her head down, ears closed, and teeth gritted, hating the way she looked. Wishing she could be like everyone else.

And suddenly, here in the city of Kyo, she *was* like everyone else. Here, she looked normal. She didn't have to steel herself against strange looks or insults. A tightness around her heart eased, and it was a wonderful feeling. She walked with an extra spring in her step, her aching feet forgotten. She smiled at passersby, and some smiled back, taking no more notice of her than any other face in the crowd. There was a delicious, exhilarating sense of effortless *belonging*.

Which lasted until the first time Hiroshi introduced her to someone and she opened her mouth.

It was three women, the wife of a ship-captain friend and two of her companions. Hiroshi literally bumped into them. They wore brightly colored coats and walked with their arms crossed and their hands tucked up into their voluminous sleeves. Their hair was done the way women of Spire wore their hair on holidays—braided and curled into elaborate coifs atop their heads, held in place against the wind with shiny pins. Hiroshi greeted them warmly. They all talked so fast Brieze had trouble picking out any words— they blurred together in a relentless rush. Hiroshi introduced her. She bowed and said in the Eastern tongue, "I am pleased to meet you, and I am enjoying my visit to your wonderful city."

But she hadn't spoken more than a few words when the women's smiles changed to the polite but pained expression people might wear at a small child's musical recital that is going badly. In the space of a few words, she'd become foreign to them.

Hiroshi repeated what she'd said. The women smiled relieved smiles and nodded. The captain's wife spoke slowly and loudly to Brieze, enunciating one word, "*Yo-koso.*"

This time, Brieze's scowl was no more than a little quirk at the corner of her mouth, quickly covered up as she bowed and said "*Arigatou.*"

Brieze sighed as the women took their leave. "Why doesn't anybody here understand me?" she asked.

"People talk very fast in Kyo," Hiroshi said, resuming their walk. "And the city dialect is different from anywhere else."

"My talking seems to offend people."

"Well, you have a very thick accent, and you mispronounce many words. And people in Kyo feel very strongly about speaking properly."

"Your crew didn't have any problems with the way I talk."

"Language is much more casual on a cargo ship. People are from many different places so there are many different ways of speaking. Also, none of my crew would dare correct you when you spoke. That would be disrespectful."

Brieze sighed. More of that wonderful respect. She walked with her shoulders hunched against the cold, mechanically trudging behind Hiroshi.

The pain in her feet came back with a vengeance.

* * *

Kyo was like Selestria in one way—its streets were a tangled mess. Hiroshi led Brieze ever upward along twisting and branching avenues and lanes, through crowded squares and open-air markets, sometimes taking a quick shortcut down alleyways so narrow she had to turn sideways to shuffle through. And no matter where they went, they were always smack in the middle of a crowd of people. *How can people live like this?* Brieze thought to herself. *If one more person bumps into me, I'm going to scream.*

When they finally reached Mama Kasshoku's boarding house, her feet were on fire. It was a large house that, like most houses in Kyo, consisted mostly of stone pillars holding up a tiled roof. There was no door. They walked between two pillars and they were inside. The house's interior was made up of flimsy looking paper partitions instead of walls. They looked to Brieze like she could easily put a fist through them. Behind some of them, shadows moved. Despite the lack of proper walls the house was warm. Several cheery fires burned in iron grates.

Hiroshi rang a bell on a stand. Footsteps stirred in the house.

Mama Kasshoku herself appeared. A thickly built, matronly woman of about forty, she wore an apron dusted with rice flour and wiped her hands with a cloth as she came. There was a dab of rice flour on her broad nose, and her salt-and-pepper hair was liberally dusted with it, too. Strands of her hair had escaped from the bun on the top of her head and stuck to her shiny forehead and cheeks. She wore a frown of disapproval as she strode toward them. A frown that seemed mostly fixed on Brieze, though she spared some for the captain. Evidently, she'd been interrupted in her preparations for the evening meal.

Mama Kasshoku pointed at Brieze's feet and said, "Tut!"

The exclamation was one of those universal sounds mothers make to reprimand children.

Brieze looked down at her feet, then up at Hiroshi. "What's wrong?" she asked.

"Ah, you should have taken off your shoes on entering the house. I'm sorry, I forgot to tell you." Hiroshi stood in bare feet. His boots were leaning against a pillar. She'd been so engrossed in studying the house's interior she hadn't seen him take them off.

"Sorry," she mumbled to Mama Kasshoku, forgetting even to try to speak in the Eastern tongue. She stepped out of her shoes.

"Ach!" Mama Kasshoku cried in horror and dismay, pointing to Brieze's feet.

Her socks were much the worse for wear after her months-long voyage. Still, they were a color you could tell had once been white. The heels and ankles, though, were soaked red with the blood of broken blisters.

Mama Kasshoku called loudly over her shoulder, barking orders that were answered by multiple voices from the house's interior.

"Hai!"

"Hai mamasan!"

She put her hands on her hips and launched into a vigorous scolding of Captain Hiroshi. Brieze didn't need a translator. The tone of her voice, her finger pointing at Brieze's feet and wagging in the captain's face, made it clear she was scolding him for being so careless as to allow a young girl to walk so far and harm her feet. Brieze bit down on a smile. It was entertaining to see Hiroshi looking like an abashed child, stammering and offering excuses which Mama Kasshoku was having none of.

"It's nothing," Brieze said. "It doesn't hurt much."

But her comment was ignored as two of the house staff bustled up, one carrying a small wooden stool, which he placed before her and invited her to sit on. The other carried a basin of steaming, soapy water, which she set near Brieze's feet.

Mama Kasshoku herself knelt to remove her socks. But she made a face as she caught a whiff of Brieze's feet, which, unfortunately, had not been properly washed during her voyage. She muttered rapidly under her breath. Brieze caught the word *banjin*. Barbarian. Mama Kasshoku stood and ordered her staff to remove Brieze's socks and wash her feet, which they did with obvious reluctance. Brieze sat there and allowed it, petrified with embarrassment. She couldn't move her mouth. Her face blazed red. Still, the warm soapy water was soothing as they placed her feet in the basin and gingerly sponged them with a cloth.

Hiroshi and Mama Kasshoku talked. Then, after giving more orders to her staff, she took her leave and marched back to the kitchen at the back of the house.

"I have arranged for you to stay here at a good price," Hiroshi said. "However, there are two conditions. First, that all your dirty clothes be laundered as soon as possible. You can leave them in a pile outside your room and the staff will wash them. For a small fee, of course."

"Fine," Brieze said. "And the second?"

"That you take a bath as soon as possible. This is being arranged in your room."

"For a small fee, of course," she said.

Hiroshi nodded. "Mama Kasshoku's is a respectable place. You'll be safe and well cared for here. This is a good neighborhood, unlike some of the unsavory neighborhoods closer to the palace where many visitors stay."

"Unsavory?"

"Rowdy taverns, brothels, opium dens. And the disreputable people who patronize them. Drinkers and thieves and worse. I don't want you exposed to that."

Brieze felt a tug of affection for the captain. He sounded like her wizard father. "Is this goodbye then?" she asked, and the thought unsettled her. Hiroshi was the only person she really knew in Kyo. The only person looking out for her.

He smiled and tousled her hair. "No, my little beast-slayer. Not goodbye. I will come by tomorrow to check on you. And once I have settled affairs with my cargo you must come to my house for dinner and meet my wife and children."

"I'd like that," she said. She was still sitting as the woman dried her feet with a towel. But she stood and gave the captain a hug.

He hugged her, then put his boots back on. "Don't forget someone from the navy will come by soon to make sure you are actually here. They'll probably ask you more questions about your stay." He bowed, flashed her one last grin, and left.

Brieze sat, and the woman finished drying her feet. The man dabbed at her broken blisters with some kind of salve. They each wrapped one of her feet in soft bandages.

"Come," the woman said in the Western tongue. "Your room."

The man picked up her backpack, which Hiroshi had left. He also picked up her dirty socks, gripping them between a thumb and forefinger as if he held the tail of a dead rat. He gestured for Brieze to follow the woman.

They led Brieze down a "hallway" of paper partitions, past "doors" that were no more than sheer silk curtains. The woman pointed to the door of Brieze's room. Brieze stepped through the curtain. The paper-walled room was tiny—a few paces long by a few paces wide. There was a bed of sorts, a thin mat on the floor with a pillow that looked like a burlap sack of grain. A low nightstand. A washstand with a pitcher and basin. A chamber pot. There was nothing like a window. Light filtered in dimly through the walls. An oil lamp and some candles sat on the nightstand.

The man set her backpack and socks on the floor. The woman asked, "Dinner here, or..." she didn't know the words. She pointed outside the room. "...there? With others."

"I'll have dinner here," Brieze said. After the embarrassments she'd already suffered, she had no desire to have dinner in the common room with Mama Kasshoku's other guests. Who knew what new indignities and mortifications awaited the *banjin* there?

"We bring bath," the woman said. "Put smelly clothes there." She wrinkled her nose rudely and pointed to the hall.

"*Arigatou*," Brieze said.

Evidently, she didn't say it right. The woman stifled a giggle. She and the man smirked at each other, made hasty bows, and ducked out of the room.

The "bath" was another basin of hot water, slightly bigger than the one they washed her feet in. They set this on the floor of Brieze's room along with a chunk of soap, washcloth, and towel. Once they'd left, she stripped, unzipping and peeling off her flightsuit and underclothes. She kept one eye on the flimsy "door" as she gave herself a vigorous sponge bath. The warm water and soap felt like a new experience to her—a priceless luxury. She stood in the basin and used the washcloth to squeeze warm water over the top of her head. That felt even better. She undid her braid, lathered up her hair, and washed away months of grime. Heavenly. She combed out the tangles until her hair fell straight and shiny like a curtain all the way down to the small of her back.

She fished out the one clean change of clothes she'd been saving from her backpack and put them on. She gathered up her dirty clothes to place in the hall outside the room. Now that she was clean, she realized how filthy the old clothes were. She sniffed them and wrinkled her nose just as the rude woman had. She blushed to remember that this pile of grubby laundry was what she'd shown up to Mama Kass-hoku's in.

Something fell out of the wad of clothes and hit the floor. Brieze stooped and picked it up. It was her mother's gray, heart-shaped stone. The one she'd slipped into her hands during the farewell on the dock. Brieze had tucked the stone into an inner pocket of her flightsuit and forgotten about it. She turned it over in her hands. It felt strangely warm. *May our love last forever*, it said. She got an odd feeling handling the stone. She felt as if someone else had been holding it, and it was still warm from their touch. She had a fleeting vision of her mother. But it was not the mother she knew. It was a young girl laughing, standing at the edge of a little churning brook. She was calling to someone, beckoning with her hands.

Voices passing in the hallway broke the spell. Brieze blinked and came back to reality. She put the dirty clothes in the hall, and she set the stone on the low table that served as a nightstand next to her bed.

Dinner was good, a fish stew with noodles and vegetables in more of that tasty coconut broth, brought in a steaming bowl on a wooden tray and set on the floor. The staff removed the basin of dirty bathwater and the clothes outside her room.

With dinner done, she lit one of the candles, got out her paper and ink, and wrote letters. She had a lot of news to tell and many people to tell it to. Her mother. Her wizard father.

Tak. She missed them all, was suddenly aware of how far away from them she was. She felt lonely. But writing letters helped, as it did before. She lay on her back in the bed, with her head propped up on the pillow, and wrote on her folded-up knees. She wrote long into the night in a pool of candle-light. When the candle burned down to a guttering squib, she blew it out, wrapped herself in the blanket, and lay her head on the pillow.

Sleep came easier than she thought it would. She thought the flimsy walls and door would make her feel exposed and vulnerable. But they offered just enough privacy and protection. Sky riders don't like to be closed in by low roofs and thick walls. In its own way, the room had a similar feel to the rooms Brieze knew because it let in plenty of air. It felt open. It allowed you to breathe. In Selestria, they accomplished this with large windows. In Kyo, they used paper walls.

Silvery moonlight filtered through the walls. The ghostly light glimmered on the heart-shaped stone on the nightstand. The carved characters stood out in sharp relief. Her eyes were drawn to it. She gazed at it, eyelids blinking and drooping. The heavy breathing and snores of other sleepers came to her through the walls.

Soon, her own slow, deep breathing joined them.

THIRTEEN

In her dream, Brieze was back on Footmont, hunting flying squirrels like she used to when she was a kid.

She flushed one out and chased it through the forest as it flitted from tree to tree. She ran with her bow in her hands, an arrow knocked. The trees were tall and thick and close. Wind rustled through their leaves. The sky was evening lavender.

The squirrel swooped, dove, hit the ground—and turned into something else. Something larger on four legs, running up the slope though the trees. Brieze ran faster, closing in on it. The sky was dimming, dusk gathering beneath the trees. She caught glimpses of her quarry—a wild boar, grunting and moving fast on its short legs. No time to stop and take aim.

The boar crashed through a tangle of underbrush and changed into something else. Something bigger, something on two feet, moving slower but still fleeing uphill, snapping branches as it went. It was fully dusk now, darkness gathering in pools on the forest floor. She couldn't make out what she chased, but she was close enough to hear its ragged breathing. It was tiring, slowing. Soon she would have it.

And then it was trapped! It ran smack into a sheer stony cliff face. No way to flee forward, and before it could turn to either side she was on it, just yards away, her bow raised and drawn, her arrow tip trained on its heart.

It was a man. He turned to face her and cowered, his hands raised in a pleading, defensive gesture. He was made of shadows. His face was a blank.

But she knew that this was her father, Kaishou Fujiwara.

✳ ✳ ✳

A woman's voice woke her. It called from outside the door to her room. "Good morning! Enter please…?"

Brieze sat up groggily in bed and mumbled something. Golden sunlight filtered in through the paper walls. The woman, the same rude one from last night, entered with a breakfast tray and set it on the floor near the bed. Although it was the same woman, her attitude was completely different. She kept her eyes respectfully lowered. And when Brieze thanked her in the Eastern language she didn't giggle or smirk at her pronunciation. She bowed gravely and left quickly on silent feet.

"Huh," Brieze said to herself. "I wonder what that's all about."

In the city of Kyo, with so many people living shoulder to shoulder, news travels fast. Yesterday, captain Hiroshi and his crew had talked often and loudly about Brieze killing the Nagmor and saving their lives. By morning, the entire city—all three mountains—knew the story. Brieze was about to get another healthy dose of the respect she loved so much.

Mama Kasshoku herself came in to examine her feet. She brought a small wooden stool, set it on the floor, and with a deferent gesture invited Brieze to sit. After looking her feet over and giving them a few experimental prods and squeezes, she seemed satisfied with their condition. "Feet like princess," she said as she squeezed them. "Soft." She applied more salve, wrapped Brieze's feet in fresh bandages, and, like her staff, bowed gravely and left quickly.

Brieze turned her attention to the breakfast. A pot of tea, milky and sweet, and spiced with all sorts of strange but pleasant flavors. She tasted clove and cardamom. There were three small fried dumplings on a plate, drizzled with honey and sprinkled with sesame seeds. They were delicious. She tried to eat them slowly, but they were gone all too soon. Her stomach rumbled as she licked honey from her fingers. The breakfast had awakened her appetite without properly satisfying it.

She recalled the smells of grilling meat and baking bread from the markets yesterday. She decided a trip to a market was in order. She needed a decent pair of shoes and thicker socks. And a heavier weight for her braid. And some new clothes, the better to blend in.

"And definitely a real breakfast," she said, braiding up her hair.

She was about to leave her room when some instinct, some little tug in her belly, made her stop and turn around.

The heart-shaped stone sat on the nightstand. She had the strong feeling that she didn't want to leave it there, alone. She picked it up and stashed it in a pocket.

✳ ✳ ✳

Brieze jostled and bumped her way through the crowded, twisting streets of Kyo, doing her best to follow the map Mama Kasshoku had sketched for her. When in doubt, she followed her nose. Eventually, she came to an open-air market that was probably the one Mama Kasshoku intended her to reach. She spotted racks of clothes and stacks of shoes at some of the vendor's stalls, set out under awnings to keep off the lightly falling snow.

"Clothes first," Brieze said, then corrected that to, "No, breakfast first."

After locating and consuming more fried dumplings drizzled with honey, and a local delicacy called egg-drop soup, which reminded her of Tak's mother's soup, she felt fortified enough to search the racks of clothing at the outdoor stands. She knew what she wanted. She'd been studying the women of Kyo ever since she'd arrived. She wanted one of those warm-looking, brightly colored padded jackets with the big shoulders and sleeves. And a matching pair of baggy trousers. But she soon discovered the clothes at the outdoor stalls were not good quality. They felt thin, and she could tell by the stitching they were not made to last.

Nosing about, she discovered an indoor clothing shop in one of the buildings bordering the open-air market. An actual shop with stone walls and a very old, slightly warped wooden door that wouldn't close all the way. A bell on the door chimed as she entered. The proprietors, a middle-aged couple, greeted her with smiles and bows. They wore brown *kimonos*, the robe-like garments, belted around the waist, that everyone wore in Kyo. Spectacles perched low on the woman's nose. A tape measure draped around the man's shoulders.

The jackets and trousers here were of much better quality. But Brieze fretted about choosing a color. All the colors—the greens, blues, reds, and yellows—were extravagantly bright and vibrant. Not really her. She'd feel like a peacock in any one of them. She found herself wishing for the muted, earthy tones popular in Spire. On the other hand, she wanted to fit in here. She'd just decided on an emerald green jacket and trousers when she spotted more clothes on a rack in the back of the store. These were all black.

Black! That was her color. She hadn't seen many people dressed in black, but there had been a few. A black outfit would allow her to fit in without feeling gaudy and uncomfortable. Quickly she selected a black jacket and trousers and brought them to the counter at the front of the store. The man's smile wavered for a moment when he saw what she'd selected. He exchanged a glance with his wife. But he remained polite as she asked the cost in the Eastern language. He didn't frown at her pronunciation. He spoke to her with simple, easy-to-understand words and phrases as he conveyed the cost and helped her find the right coins from her purse.

But as Brieze counted out the coins, the man's brow wrinkled anxiously. Something was bothering him. Before the sale was final he said, "You sure you want black? Many other pretty colors for pretty young woman."

"Yes," Brieze said. But she understood from the man's nervous tone that more than just a fashion choice was at stake here. "Is something wrong with black?"

The man conferred with his wife in whispered undertones. Finally he said, "Black color only for…important people."

Ah, that was it. Brieze remembered. In the Eastern Kingdoms black was reserved for people of high station. High-ranking government officials, nobles, scholars of exceptional note. In some parts of the Eastern Kingdoms it was actually illegal for people to wear black without official permission. She couldn't remember if Kyo was one of those places or not.

Should she choose another color?

The answer came to her from within. If she were going to meet with the Fujiwaras, she needed to look important. She needed to remind them she was the apprentice of a powerful wizard, not some young girl to be taken lightly. She wasn't going to ask permission to wear black of anyone. She would assume it as her right. And if they wanted to challenge her, or arrest her, well they were welcome to try. She drew herself up to her full height and gave the man her best, black-eyed, glittering, Nagmor-slayer look.

"Black," she said.

"Black," he agreed meekly.

* * *

As she navigated the crowded streets back to Mama Kasshoku's, Brieze's stomach rumbled, reminding her it was past lunchtime. She wore her new black trousers tucked into a comfortable pair of fur-lined black boots. Her new jacket felt crisp and snug and warm. The silver-gilded buttons down its front gleamed in the winter sun. Her breath came out in cloudy puffs. A light snow fell, the flakes catching in her hair. She carried a sturdy duffel bag with a strap over one shoulder. She'd bought it to hold her new belongings, and her old. In it were her old clothes and shoes, several pairs of new warm socks, and a jade and silver weight for her braid which she was sure she paid too much for but didn't care.

She had an excellent, almost eidetic, memory. She recalled every twist and turn that had led her from Mama Kasshoku's to the market, and she had no problem retracing her route. She also remembered the location of every stand selling grilled meats, and she stopped at several of these on her way back, buying small portions of mouth-wateringly fragrant, spiced meat on wooden skewers and eating as she walked. Some tasted more like fowl, some more like fish. They were all delicious.

As she walked, rubbing shoulders with the masses of Kyo, she again enjoyed that easing around her heart, that dropping of her old defenses. Nothing about her attracted anyone's attention or marked her as different. No one gave her a second glance. Some even offered her friendly smiles. Every face was like her own, familiar in a way. She felt herself blending in, and relaxed into a peaceful sense of anonymity. She felt as if she were light, floating, barely there—a bird about to take flight on the next wintry breeze.

Which lasted until she got back to Mama Kasshoku's.

The first thing she noticed as she approached the house was a large airship hovering directly above it. The crew were executing a hovering maneuver exactly like the one Tak had taught her. She wondered if it were an unusual thing to have a large airship hovering over Mama Kasshoku's, and she guessed that it was, judging from the number of people who'd come out into the street to stare at it.

The next thing she noticed was Mama Kasshoku standing out in front of the house as if she were waiting. An official-looking man in a gray navy uniform stood next to Mama Kasshoku as if he, too, were waiting.

Mama Kasshoku introduced the man. She spoke in the Eastern tongue, in a rush. Brieze didn't catch the man's name but she got most of his title. Something along the lines of military liaison to the diplomatic service. Or possibly diplomatic liaison to the military service. In any case, the man spoke fluently in the Western tongue.

"Greetings," he said, bowing. "May I presume you are Lady Brieze, apprentice to Wizard Radolphus of the Kingdom of Spire, and we have the honor of your visit to the city of Kyo?"

"That is correct," Brieze said, straightening her shoulders. Everyone in the street stopped staring at the airship and stared at her instead.

"And am I also correct in understanding you desire an audience with Takashi Fujiwara?"

Brieze blinked, taken aback. She knew from what Hiroshi had told her that Takashi Fujiwara was head of the clan, ruler of Kyo and the mountains of Onshu. "I had hoped to meet with someone from the Fujiwara clan," she said, "but I wouldn't presume to request an audience with Mr. Takashi."

"Well, he would very much like to meet with you."

Brieze swallowed. This was all happening extremely fast. And not how she imagined it at all. "I would be honored," she said, a bit breathlessly. "When?"

The man grinned and cocked an eye up at the airship. Already, the crew was lowering a rope ladder with wooden rungs. "Why, now, of course," he said.

✳   ✳   ✳

The Emperor's Palace crowned the tallest of Kyo's three mountains, called simply Big Kyomont. From the deck of the approaching ship, the palace looked to Brieze like a giant, elaborate layer cake. At the bottom, a foundation of pillars held up an ornate roof. This roof in turn supported another, slightly smaller, set of pillars and a roof, and these another, and so on and so on as the palace rose into the sky.

The ship docked at the palace quay, a stone structure just like those at the port, jutting from the mountain below the palace. Brieze and the liaison official disembarked. He led

her up steep stone steps, through the palace's main gate—
past guards who nodded deferentially—then along a laby-
rinth of hallways and stairways until they entered the Emperor's throne room.

The Emperor was not at residence in the palace. He occupied a palace in the mountains of Kaido to the north, leaving Takashi Fujiwara to manage his affairs in Kyo and the
mountains of Onshu. Exactly why this was so, Brieze wasn't
certain, but she didn't doubt it had to do with the political
maneuverings of the Fujiwaras.

The Emperor's throne room was not so different from its
counterpart in Castle Selestria. A forest of tree-sized pillars
held up a roof far, far above. The walls were stone here—
paper could never keep out the mountaintop winds—and
massive windows, closed against the winter chill, let in
streams of sunlight. But Takashi Fujiwara did not sit on the
throne. That would be too presumptuous, even for him. The
man led Brieze to a side room, one of the suite of rooms that
Takashi Fujiwara and his staff used as offices and meeting
rooms.

There were no chairs. Easterners didn't seem to use
chairs. Takashi Fujiwara sat on a plump cushion in the center of the room, in front of a low table set with a tea service.
His wife Emiko sat beside him. They both wore black silk
kimonos, embroidered with gold and silver dragons. Their
faces were fleshy in the way of those used to good food and
comfort, and their eyes were calm and heavy-lidded in the
way of those accustomed to power. Brieze guessed they
were about her grandparents' age. Takashi had a thin black

mustache and goatee. Emiko's hair was done up in an elaborate coif held together with jeweled pins. Her face was powdered white, with rouged cheeks and lips, as was the custom among aristocratic women.

A servant invited Brieze to sit, poured tea for everyone, and disappeared. She sat face-to-face with the Fujiwaras. *This is it*, she said to herself, and she kicked herself for not having rehearsed anything to say. She'd thought she would have more time. As with her farewell speech, she was going to have to wing it. And she remembered how well that went.

Fortunately, they engaged her in small talk first. And they used the Western tongue, which they both spoke fairly well. They asked her politely how old she was, where she lived. They asked many questions about the wizard's community and the floating island. Then they asked her about her journey, and especially about the encounter with the Nagmor. They made her recount the entire adventure in great detail. Brieze answered honestly, and as well as she could. As she talked, the Fujiwaras looked at her as if she were some strange new chess piece that had appeared on their board, and they were trying to figure out how it moved.

Takashi cleared his throat. "So, you killed the beast with nothing more than two small bombs that fit in the palms of your hands?"

"That is correct, your eminence," Brieze said.

"We would be very interested to have these bombs, or know how they could be made. They would provide great protection to our ships."

Brieze hesitated. She had not expected this request, although she should have. The bombs were her wizard father's own private invention, and not part of the technology wizards had decided to share with others. Although he had not expressly forbidden it, she knew she could not simply hand over the bombs to the Easterners. That would violate wizard law. She explained this, as well as she could. But she also knew an absolute refusal would not be polite or correct, and it wouldn't get her anywhere with the Fujiwaras.

"I would be pleased to write the wizard and ask him," she said. "And to share this technology if he approves." She knew he would say no, and she expected the Fujiwaras knew it too, but it was the best she could offer.

"That would be well," Takashi said, and switched his line of questioning. "So tell us, what brings you to our city?"

Brieze swallowed. Her mouth went dry. This was really it. Time to just muddle through.

"I came here to find a man named Kaishou Fujiwara, who traveled to the West seventeen years ago in a merchant ship called the *Atago Maru*," she said.

The Fujiwaras instantly tensed up. They exchanged glances, then looked at her as if she were a strange new chess piece that had just made a puzzling, potentially threatening, move.

"And why, may I ask, are you looking for him?" Takashi asked.

Brieze forced the words out of her dry mouth. "I believe he is my father."

Takashi and Emiko gasped as one. And not just the two

of them. Brieze heard a third surprised gasp in the room. Her eyes darted to where it came from. The gasp came from behind an ornate paper screen, adorned with drawings of lotus flowers and peacocks, set up in a corner of the room. From behind the screen, a wooden chair creaked.

There was a dreadful uncomfortable silence.

"What do you want?" Takashi finally said, his lips tight and his tone edged with anger.

"Nothing..." Brieze stammered. "Just to meet with him...and ask him some questions."

"You come here claiming to be the daughter of a Fuji-wara. And you make claims to shame us. Is it money you want? Do you think to blackmail us? Do you have any proof?"

"No proof," Brieze said. "Just what my mother told me."

Takashi and Emiko talked fast and low in the Eastern tongue. Brieze caught none of it.

"You will leave now," Takashi said. "You are no longer welcome in the Eastern Kingdoms. You must return home. Guards! Come in here. Escort this woman to—"

"Wait!" came a voice from behind the paper screen.

Takashi and Emiko paused. The guards, who'd just entered the room, paused too.

The wooden chair creaked again. And then, by slow degrees, and old woman emerged from behind the screen. Her back was bent, and she used a cane to walk. She wore a plain black kimono. Her face was cracked and ancient. Her silver hair was cut short like a monk's. Nobody moved as the old woman shuffled up to Brieze, her cane wobbling with each step. She peered directly into Brieze's face. She wore spectacles that made her fiercely intelligent eyes look huge as she studied Brieze's features. She gripped Brieze's chin with gnarled fingers and turned her head to the left, then the right. Finally, she stood back with a grunt and leaned on her cane.

"You are dismissed," she said to the guards. They vanished in an instant, closing the door behind them.

"Takashi," the old woman said, "bring me my chair."

He jumped up and fetched the chair from behind the screen. He set it behind the old woman and held her elbow as she creakily lowered herself into it.

"You are fools," she said, folding her hands atop her cane. "Even my old eyes can she is the image of Kaishou. She has his eyes. His nose. And his build." She looked Brieze up and down. "Tall and spindly. Like a crane."

"Even so," Takashi said. "We cannot—"

"Silence," the old woman said. "I want to hear what Kaishou was up to all those years ago in the West. I want to hear the girl's story. So my little crane, speak."

Brieze took a breath, wet her lips with a sip of tea, and told the story as her mother had told it to her.

When she finished, Takashi said, "This tale, if true, dishonors us."

Anger welled up in Brieze. "It was my *mother* who was dishonored. And come to think of it, I do have proof of a sort." Brieze took her mother's heart-shaped stone from an inner pocket. "If the tale is true, Kaishou will recognize this stone. My mother said he inscribed it and gave it to her. Let me show it to him and see what he has to say."

The old woman extended a hand for the stone. Brieze

gave it to her. She examined it, turning it over in her hands. "He never should have gone on that voyage," she said softly. "He was no merchant, no adventurer. He was a scholar. He had a head for mathematics and science, not airships and trading."

"It is a son's duty to do as his father commands, not as he would please," Takashi said. "Though if I had a second chance, I would have let him stay and continue his studies."

"And as my son, you will do as *I* command," the old woman said. "We will not throw the girl out like a beggar or a thief. We will take her in as a guest of the palace."

Brieze's eyes flitted from the old woman to Takashi. She wasn't sure if she was following the conversation correctly.

The old woman sighed. "And there may be no dishonor. We can never know for certain," she handed the stone to Brieze and leaned back in her chair. "My dear little crane, I regret to tell you this, but the *Atago Maru* never returned from that voyage seventeen years ago. Nor did any of her crew."

"The ship was lost," Takashi said, his voice husky with years of grief. "With all hands aboard."

Brieze sat there blinking, stunned.

Kaishou Fujiwara was dead.

And the ancient woman who sat before her was, evidently, her great grandmother.

Takashi and Emiko were her grandparents.

Tears glimmered in the old woman's eyes. "Still, something of Kaishou has returned to us after all these years. It is a miracle, a gift beyond any we could have hoped for, and a cause for joy."

FOURTEEN

Tak squatted in the bow of the *Arrow*, trying to shift some of the supplies in the bow storage compartment, when Jon cleared his throat and spoke.

"I see something," he said.

Tak jumped up, startled. This was the first complete sentence Jon had uttered all day. It signaled that something important, or unusual, was up. In the weeks they'd been traveling together, Tak had come to realize just how little Jon actually spoke. The scrawny giant stood in the stern, gazing westward behind them through his spyglass. Tak moved aft to join him, and scanned the sky with his own glass. The wind whipped their hair and tugged at their cloaks. Snowflakes whirled in the air. Their breath came out in cloudy puffs. The *Arrow* pitched and rocked on the current.

There it was! A sail. A silvery sail glinting in what little gray light filtered through the clouds of the Eastern Emptiness. Even at the extreme distance, Tak could tell by the way the sail glimmered that it was made of pure spider silk, just like the *Arrow's* own sail. It wasn't one of those second-rate jobs with vlisken fibers woven in. That meant the owner of the craft—for it clearly was a small craft, propelled by a single sail—had money. Tak gazed at it for a long time, straining his eyes, trying to discover anything more about it. It was the first ship of any kind they'd seen since they entered the Emptiness.

"It's changed course," Tak said. "It's heading straight for us. And it's gaining on us."

Jon grunted in agreement. He chewed the beard under his lower lip. Then, with a sound like a rhinoceros suffering from a bad head cold, he snorted up an enormous quantity of phlegm and spit it over the side. The wintry chill made his nose run and clog, and that was how he cleared it.

Tak made a face and bit down on a snide remark. Jon's near-perpetual silence, broken only by his grunting and that awful noise he made before spitting wads of mucus out into the Eastern Emptiness, was getting on his nerves. In fact, in the time they'd traveled together, Tak had discovered many things about Jon that annoyed him. The way he picked his teeth with his pinky fingernail after they ate. The way the dried beans they cooked gave him pungent gas, which he passed loudly, and often, and especially at night, when they slept side to side in the cramped space of the *Arrow's* weather shelter. And Jon was irritated by many of the things that Tak did, especially his constant fussing over the balance of the ship, his continual, obsessive shifting of their supplies from one place to another. But there was no escaping each other. The *Arrow* was only eighteen feet long, its deck eight feet wide. The close quarters provided plenty of opportunities for the boys to grate on each other. The ever-increasing cold and lousy, mostly cold food didn't help either.

Tak took a step backward and stumbled, nearly tripping over Jon's axe, which he'd left lying around on the deck—again.

"Dammit!" Tak said. "I keep telling you, put this thing somewhere out of the way."

The axe was another thing that annoyed Tak. It was a stupid, clunky, heavy thing to have aboard an airship. There was no good place to stow it, and wherever Jon tried to stow it, it always managed to get loose and slide around the deck. Tak was extremely sensitive to the weight and balance of the *Arrow*, and he could *feel* that ridiculously big iron axe head throwing things off. He fantasized about tossing the axe overboard. Sometimes, he fantasized about tossing Jon along with it.

Jon picked up the axe and gave Tak one of his eloquent looks. *I know where I'd like to put it.* He stowed the axe in one of the side compartments along the gunwale, but of course it didn't fit. Half the handle stuck out.

Tak was irritated for another reason that had little to do with Jon. The *Arrow*, crammed full and weighed down with supplies, felt like a completely different ship. It responded sluggishly to the tiller. It rode the currents heavily. It was *slow*. The fact this mystery ship was gaining on them was proof of that.

Jon raised his spyglass again and fixed it on the ship behind them. He frowned and made a belligerent growl in the back of this throat. "Pirates?" he said.

Tak had been wondering the same thing. Jon voicing the

thought made the possibility seem more real. The fact the ship had changed course and was clearly intent on overtaking them didn't bode well. And pirates—good ones at least—definitely had money. They could afford spider silk sails.

"We'll know soon enough," Tak said. "If it is pirates, there can't be many of them. It looks like just a two-man ship." Of course, it could be a scouting party, with a bigger ship lurking somewhere just over the horizon. The mystery ship was close enough now that the boys could see it without their spyglasses. It was directly astern of them. Still gaining.

"I'm getting my axe," Jon said. "No pirate's gonna set foot on this ship without me doing something about it."

"Yes, let's have some weapons handy," Tak said. "Just in case."

* * *

As the ship approached within hailing distance, Tak crouched in the stern with his quiver of arrows slung over his shoulder, gripping his bow. He had an arrow nocked and the bow at half draw. Jon crouched next to him, gripping his axe with white-knuckled hands.

"Ho there!" Tak shouted, raising his bow and aiming his arrow at the ship. "Identify yourself or we will fire on you!"

For a long moment no answer came.

Then a man shouted back. "We're looking for Taktinius Spinner junior. Are you him?"

Tak and Jon exchanged surprised looks. Tak relaxed the draw of his bow.

"Maybe," he shouted. "Who are you?"

"Your father sent us. We have something for you."

The mystery ship glided up to the *Arrow*, so close their hulls rasped together and their sails overlapped above them. Tak could see now that the ship was a messenger ship, built to be very light and fast. It was the kind of ship commonly used to ferry letters and information from mountain to mountain in the Kingdom of Spire. It had a crew of two. One man stood in the bow as the ship approached. The other worked the tiller and pedals in the stern. Tak caught glimpses of messenger livery underneath their cloaks.

"Thank the winds we found you!" the man in the bow said as he hopped onto the *Arrow* without asking permission to come aboard. "I didn't fancy spending any more time out here looking for you."

Jon of course said nothing. But his eyes blinked and his nose twitched inquisitively as he leaned on his axe.

Tak was too surprised to say anything more than "My father sent you...?" Sending a messenger ship out into the Eastern Emptiness to chase down another ship was not something that was done every day. In fact, it wasn't done at all.

"He did," the man said, grinning. "And he paid us well. He wanted us to give you this."

The man handed him an old logbook with a well-worn oilskin cover. Inside, there was a folded navigational chart of the Eastern Emptiness and the Eastern Kingdoms. There was also a note.

> *Tak,*
> *This book and chart are from my voyage to the Eastern Kingdoms, when I wasn't much older than you are now. I hope they will be helpful to you.*
> *I regret my harsh words at our last meeting. My only wish is for you to return home safely.*
> *Your Father*

Tak swallowed down a lump in his throat. His eyes glistened. "How did he look?" he asked. "When you saw him?"

"He looked good," the man said, though there was a note of false cheer in his voice. "Definitely on the mend. He'll be riding the currents again in no time."

Tak took a deep breath and let it out with a sigh. He, too, regretted his harsh words. And his actions. He very much wished he could see his father for himself. He wondered how he was faring, and what he was doing.

＊　＊　＊

Taktinius Spinner senior lay in bed with the covers pulled up to his bearded chin. He listened for sounds of his wife in the house, trying to determine where she was and what she was doing. Late-morning sunlight slanted through the windows. He strained his ears for any sound, and finally heard a chair scrape on the floor in the kitchen below. Then the unmistakable sound of a knife chopping vegetables on a wooden block. Good. That meant she'd be staying put for a while.

He groaned as he pulled himself up, threw off the covers, and sat on the edge of the bed. He felt lightheaded, and that small exertion brought perspiration to his upper lip. He took several deep breaths. Finally, he climbed completely out of bed, knelt on the floor, reached under the bed, and retrieved the chamber pot.

"My love?" Marghorettia called from below. "Are you up?"

"Yes my love," he croaked back.

"Don't forget to take your medicine."

"I'm doing it now, my love."

He uncorked the big bottle of greenish stuff on the night stand and poured a spoonful. But instead of taking the medicine, he tipped the spoonful into the chamber pot. He'd been getting rid of the stuff this way for more than a week now. He re-corked the bottle, and he was careful to lick the last of the medicine from the spoon. That way, his wife would taste it on his lips if she kissed him, and she would see the spoon had been used. Her sharp senses and keen mind missed very little that went on in the Spinner house.

He used the chamber pot and slid it back underneath the bed.

Now it was time to start his day. He had several tasks to complete. His brother Julius would be arriving at noon. Julius had been filling in for him as Chief Sailspinner, and they had important matters to discuss—especially the final tallies for the spider silk harvest on Silkmont, and the readiness of the factory in Selestria, which had suffered damage during the siege, for spinning the priceless silvery stuff into sails. Tak senior had some reports and correspondence to read to prepare for the meeting. These lay on his desk in his office, at the top story of the house.

He washed up with the pitcher of water and basin on the nightstand. He threw a dressing gown over his nightshirt and stepped into a pair of slippers. It was only Julius, so no use getting fully dressed. He took up the cane that leaned against the nightstand and, moving slowly, leaning heavily on the cane, headed for the stairs.

The wooden stairs creaked unnecessarily loudly as he climbed, one step at a time, firmly planting his cane and hauling himself up each step. He stopped and rested after only half-a-dozen steps. His head swam. Dark spots danced before his eyes. His breath came in ragged gulps, and his leg blazed with pain as if the Gublin sword that stabbed him were still there, buried in the flesh of his thigh. He felt the wound with his fingers through his gown. It was tender, swollen, and hot.

"Are you all right, my love?" Marghorettia called.

He wiped the sweat off his brow with a sleeve. "Perfectly fine, my dear."

He looked up. So many stairs yet to go. He pulled himself together and hauled himself up another step. And another. His arm trembled. His legs didn't want to obey him.

"I'm coming up there," Marghorettia announced.

He opened his mouth to tell her not to come, that he was fine, but never spoke the words. The dark spots dancing before his eyes coalesced into blackness. The cane slipped from his fingers. His legs buckled. He collapsed and slid to the bottom of the stairs.

FIFTEEN

Brieze moved into the palace as a guest. The plan was for her to spend the winter in Kyo and return home in the spring. The Fujiwaras put out the word that she was an honored visitor, the apprentice of a powerful wizard. They did not mention she was Kaishou's daughter, a Fujiwara herself, and they made her promise to keep the secret as well. She slept in a spacious stone room with glass windows and a canopied bed. She had the run of the palace, and she dined most evenings with the Fujiwaras. The *Devious* was brought to the castle quay. Brieze was given a permit to fly whenever she wished.

Captain Hiroshi kept his word and invited her to dinner at his house. He had two rambunctious children, a boy of seven and a girl of eight. His wife was younger and prettier than Brieze expected. The wife felt the same way about Brieze, judging from the displeased, suspicious looks she shot Brieze across the table when she thought she wasn't looking. Looks that said, *So you are the pretty young thing that slept in my husband's bed and shared his meals? If I find out anything happened…* Brieze wished she could have explained it wasn't like that.

Hiroshi had obtained all the old aeronautical records pertaining to the *Atago Maru*. He spread them out on the table after dinner was finished and the children had been put to bed. He and Brieze poured through them. They concentrated on a report of the investigation that was made into the ship's disappearance.

"This is the last recorded sighting," Hiroshi said, tapping a page of the report with a finger. "The *Atagu Maru* traded news with another merchant ship as it was heading home, two days out from the Wind's Teeth. The captain said he intended to take the middle passage, the same one we took."

"Then the *Atago Maru* wrecked in the Teeth," Brieze said.

"Or they were attacked by pirates," Hiroshi said. "That is what the report concludes."

"If they were attacked by pirates, what would have happened to the crew?"

"Killed or sold as slaves."

"If Kaishou was sold as a slave, might he still be alive?"

Hiroshi shook his head grimly. "I'm afraid slaves don't live that long. They are worked and starved to death. Most last only a year or two. Certainly not seventeen years."

"How do you know that?"

Hiroshi stroked his beard. "Admittedly, these are only rumors. No slave has ever escaped from the Dragonlord's realm. But the rumors come from the pirates who sell the slaves, so I believe them."

Brieze chewed her lower lip and pondered. So her father had either perished in the Wind's Teeth, and his remains lay in the wreck of the *Atago Maru,* or he had died a slave in the Dragonlord's realm. She imagined returning home and telling this to her mother. It wouldn't do. It didn't answer the crucial question—had Kaishou intended to keep his promise and return to her mother, or had their romance been just a bit of fun for him?

She needed to answer that question, somehow.

When she dined with the Fujiwaras, she asked countless questions about Kaishou, and asked for stories about him. The stories painted a different picture than the one she'd had in her head. She had always imagined Kaishou as a drinker and a womanizer, the kind of man with a girl in every port. But according to the Fujiwaras, he was a quiet, serious boy, dedicated to his studies at the university. He didn't frequent taverns, and he had few friends. He spent most of his time attending lectures at the university or studying in his room, reading late into the night by the light of an oil lamp.

"The boy hardly left his room. He was eighteen years old and he'd barely been outside the city of Kyo," Takashi said one night as he passed Brieze a platter of dumplings. "That is why I made him take that voyage. I wanted him to see something of the world, to experience *life.*"

"It would appear that he did," said the old woman, her great grandmother, looking at Brieze with a mixture of amusement and affection as she sipped her tea. The woman's name was Mizuki.

A thought occurred to Brieze, and she asked Emiko, "Did Kaishou write any letters home from his voyage?"

Emiko glanced at Mizuki, who nodded.

"He wrote several letters, and I have kept them," Emiko said. "But they were all written before his ship arrived in the West. We have no letters from him after that."

"Clearly, he was preoccupied with other matters," Takashi said.

"What about a diary, or a journal?" Brieze asked. "Did he keep one of those?"

"He kept a journal," Emiko said. "He wrote in it every day. But he would never let anyone see it."

"Is it here?"

"No. It was not in his room. Most certainly, he brought it with him on the voyage."

"So if he had it with him, he might have written in it about my mother," Brieze said.

There was a long silence at the table.

Takashi cleared his throat, "That journal, if it survived, would be with his remains and his personal effects in the wreck of the *Atago Maru*. Beneath the surface clouds in the great graveyard of ships strewn about the roots of the Wind's Teeth. It might as well be on the moon."

Brieze chewed her lower lip as she fiddled with the food on her plate, still trying to get used to using two wooden sticks instead of a fork. A plan was taking shape in her mind.

Mizuki narrowed her shrewd, bespectacled eyes at Brieze and frowned. "Don't even *think* about it," she said. "A young girl scouting around under the clouds at the roots of the Wind's Teeth? In the wintertime? You'd join your father's bones down there for sure."

"And there are an untold number of wrecks down there," Takashi said. "You would never find the *Atago Maru*, even if you knew where to begin looking."

Oh but I would, Brieze thought. *I know exactly how.*
And I will.

* * *

Brieze spent the next week exploring the city, both on foot and by air. She told the Fujiwaras that she was sightseeing, and she *did* actually see some sights—the great temple on Little Kyomont, the Library of Kyo with its staggeringly huge collection of books and scrolls—but what she was really doing was gathering supplies and loading them up in the *Devious*. For a trip to the Teeth and back, she needed as much food and water as the ship could hold. And there were several other things, some very specific things, that she needed to put her plan into place.

She transferred her clothes and personal things in her palace room little by little to the *Devious*, so that she wouldn't be seen leaving the palace with a fully loaded pack on the night she slipped away. Her room grew suspiciously emptier and emptier, but nobody but the palace room keepers noticed, she supposed.

On the night she planned to leave, she wrote a letter to Mizuki, Takashi, and Emiko. She apologized for sneaking away. She was sure her new family would try to stop her. They had discussed the idea no further after that first night, but she knew that *they* knew she was thinking about it. It broke her heart to leave them like this, after they had been so kind to her. Part of her letter said:

> *You once said my arrival was a gift to you. Please know that finding you has been a gift to me. I have cherished our time together, and I will return to Kyo as soon as possible with any more information I have before returning to Spire in the spring.*

She left the letter on the night stand in her room. Kaishou's heart-shaped stone sat there. She picked it up and tucked it into an inner pocket. She looked around, checking for any last little thing she'd forgotten. She wore her black flight suit, and she pulled on her padded black jacket over it. She shouldered the small duffle bag she'd bought at the market, packed with her last few things. Her heart was heavy. This felt like leaving home, and a betrayal.

If she knew her new family a little better, she would have known she wouldn't be getting away quite so easily.

She nodded casually to the palace guards as she strolled out of the main entrance. They nodded back. She made her way down to the quay where the *Devious* was docked. She tried to move at an unhurried pace, but her heart beat faster, and she grew uncomfortably warm in her flight suit and winter jacket, despite the wintery air.

The sun had just set, but still the quay was busy. Airships of every size and description were docking or taking off. The air traffic above Kyo did not lessen with the coming of night. Ships flew with bright lanterns at their bow and stern. Brieze paused to take in the view of the city of Kyo at night. On all three mountains, the lights of the city mixed with the dazzling, dancing lights in the air. It looked like fireflies swarming above the city. She sighed, adjusted the bag on her shoulder, and made her way down the steps to the quay.

The quay was crowded with throngs of people. They moved in and out of pools of light cast by oil lanterns lit and hauled up tall poles. A knot of shadowy people were gathered right where the *Devious* was docked. Brieze cursed this under her breath, but then she reasoned it wouldn't matter if she was seen taking off from the quay. As far as anyone knew, she was just another night flier, off on some evening errand.

As she came closer, she saw the knot of people were palace guards. And they were all looking at her. Her throat tightened. As she moved to within speaking distance, the group of guards parted to reveal Takashi, Emiko, and Mizuki standing in their midst, eyeing Brieze accusingly.

"You would leave us without saying goodbye?" Mizuki asked. She stood as straight as she could, with both hands perched atop her cane. She looked strange and out of place standing on the quay, wrapped in a black cloak. Brieze had never seen her outside of the palace before. In fact, Mizuki almost never left it.

Brieze stammered, "I'm not going anywhere grandmother. Just out for a night flight…to see the city lights."

Takashi harrumphed. "In a ship loaded with *months* of food and supplies? All in secret?"

"And you've cleaned out your room," Emiko said.

Brieze's shoulders slumped. Despite the winter chill, she was burning up inside her layers of clothes. But she straightened up defiantly, realizing something. "You've been spying on me!"

Mizuki shrugged. "We had people keeping an eye on you," she said. "For your own protection. Kyo is not the safest place for a young woman to wander alone."

Brieze crossed her arms and arched an eyebrow skeptically.

"And yes, we were spying. Be reasonable my little crane. It's what we do."

"Are you going to try to stop me?" Brieze asked, eyeing the guards, sizing up her chances of an escape, which were pretty much nil.

"Yes!" Takashi stepped forward. "You can't go wandering around the roots of the Wind's Teeth in winter, looking for a shipwreck. You'll never find it. You'll freeze to death, or starve to death, first. No one should even *be* down there in the first place."

"I'll be fine," Brieze said. "I've been to the underworld before. I have all the equipment and supplies I need. And I have a plan for finding the *Atagu Maru*."

It was Emiko's turn to cross her arms and arch a skeptical eyebrow. "What plan?" she asked.

Brieze explained it to them. Their faces grew more and more astonished—and fearful—as she laid out the details.

"You can't be serious," Emiko said. Her face had gone even paler under her powdered cheeks.

"It's suicide," Takashi said. "We can't let you go. Our

guards will take you back to the palace by force if necessary. We'll lock you up until you come to your senses."

"Silence!" Mizuki held up a hand. "Ever the hothead and fool, Takashi. Would you kidnap a citizen of Spire and hold her against her will? The apprentice of their wizard, no less? Would you turn our long-time friends and allies against us, and risk war? No, the girl must be allowed to go if we can't convince her to stay."

"Then I'm going," Brieze said.

Mizuki held out a gnarled hand to Brieze. Brieze took it. Mizuki's eyes glistened as she looked up at her great grand-daughter. "Please," she said, her tone soft and helpless with that special kind of helplessness that comes from a parent's love. "Please don't do this thing. Please stay."

Brieze swallowed hard. She put her arms around the old woman. Mizuki hugged her back with all the strength she could put into her frail limbs. They held each other for a long time, until Brieze gently broke the embrace and held Mizuki at arm's length.

"I must go," she said.

Mizuki fought down the tears threatening to brim over in her eyes. She held herself as erect and stoically as she could. "Then we wish you well," she said hoarsely. "And we will watch the skies for your return."

With a heart so heavy it sank into her boots, Brieze embraced Emiko and Takashi as well. She climbed into the *Devious*. The guards were courteous enough to undo her mooring lines and shove her off as she raised the sail. The sail stretched full and the ship rose on the wind. Brieze watched her new family grow smaller and smaller as she climbed higher, their upturned faces becoming less and less distinct. Finally, they blended into the other shadowy figures of people on the quay, and then the quay blended into the other lights of the city.

Mizuki, Takashi, and Emiko stood together on the quay, watching a small ship the color of night vanish into the sky.

Emiko buried her head in Takashi's shoulder. "We will never see her again," she said.

Mizuki wiped at her eyes. "I have a feeling we will," she said. "I hate to admit it, but I think her plan just might work."

SIXTEEN

The month-long solo trip out to the Teeth was not nearly as bad as the first leg of her voyage had been. Brieze knew what to expect this time, and she prepared herself. She brought several books with her. Eastern books written in the eastern language; long, epic tales of princesses and princes, dragons and sorcerers. They kept her mind occupied and sharpened up her language skills at the same time. And, most importantly, she brought a large bag of candies. They were eastern candies with strange flavors like ginger and co-conut and sesame, but they did the trick.

Approaching the Wind's Teeth all on her own was daunting. They looked even bigger than she remembered, which didn't seem possible since they were the biggest things she'd ever seen. But there they were, impossibly gargantuan, and menacing, and glittering with the light of the rising sun. Brieze nosed the *Devious* into the middle passage. She didn't intend to go far in. Hopefully not far enough to have to wrestle with the Teeth's treacherous winds. Just far enough in to find a place to set the *Devious* down.

She searched for half a day before finding what she was

looking for—a broad ledge jutting out from near the base of one of the Teeth, just above the surface clouds and big enough for her to set the *Devious* down without too much trouble. She furled the sail and anchored the ship with long steel anchoring stakes, pounded into the ledge with a heavy hammer. The semi-translucent, crystal-like stone was brittle and flaky, but she pounded the stakes in deep, and they held.

To her surprise, the *Devious* turned black. She'd expected the ship to turn white, which would have been the best color for camouflage. But the Teeth were made of translucent crystal. They had no color themselves, although they reflected a multitude of colors, just like a diamond. Evidently, in the absence of a predominant color, the ship's pigment went black. That made sense to Brieze in a way, since black was the absence of color, at least according to the science of optics. But she didn't like it at all. It meant the ship contrasted sharply with the ledge and could easily be spotted from the air, if anyone were looking.

She discovered a large, crack-like cave at the rear of the ledge. She didn't like this either. Such caves were used by pirates. She considered searching for a different ledge, but she might not find one by nightfall. So she investigated the cave. It had once been used by *someone*. She found the charred remains of a cooking fire, with old chicken bones and apple cores strewn around it. The apple cores were withered and dry, but they hadn't rotted. Almost nothing lived in the environment of the Teeth, and she supposed that went for the microscopic creatures that caused rot and decay. She was glad to have evidence of this. It made it more likely she'd find Kaishou's journal intact, if she could find it.

She unpacked gear from the *Devious*. She took out a long coil of sturdy rope—six hundred feet long, with thick knots tied in it at three-foot intervals. She tied one end to an anchoring stake and drove it deeply into the rock, making sure it held tight. She tied the other end to a heavy backpack loaded with a tent and all the supplies she would need during her time in the underworld. With some lighter rope, she lashed a small bundle of firewood and a sack of dried goat meat to the pack. She rummaged through the pack and took out a slim glass cylinder, two feet long, filled with liquid. She shook the rod hard until it glowed with bluish light. She fastened the light stick to the pack with a strap.

She looked over the ledge. The clouds that covered the roots of the Wind's Teeth were only a few yards below her, looking like gray mist. She used the sturdy rope with the knots to lower the pack over the ledge, foot-by-foot down through the mist, toward the unseen ground below. As she let out the rope hand-over-hand, she made a mental calculation every time ten knots went by. Thirty feet…sixty feet… ninety feet…one-hundred twenty feet…

The glowing light stick on the pack dimmed as it descended through the fog. Brieze hoped her rope was long enough.

A hundred knots passed…three hundred feet. And still the pack dangled heavily from the rope. The light had been completely swallowed up by the fog. Three-hundred sixty feet…three-ninety…four-hundred twenty feet….

At one-hundred and seventy knots—five-hundred and ten feet—the rope went slack. The pack had reached the bottom! With ninety feet to spare.

Brieze readied herself for a five-hundred foot climb down to the roots of the Wind's Teeth. She fastened metal climbing shoes with sharp metal cleats to the soles of her boots. She pulled on a pair of thick leather gloves. The worst part was getting herself over the ledge. She walked backward to the very edge, leaning on her rope, trusting it to hold her. Then she leaned back a little more and took one step over and down. Her cleats held. The rope held. She took another step and then she was standing out from the side of the tooth, her feet planted firmly on it, the rope holding her entire weight.

She walked herself down, using footholds where she could to take the strain off the rope and her arms. The wind whipped her braid back and forth. She wished she'd remembered to tuck it away, but there was nothing she could do about it now. She counted the knots as they went by, calculating how far she'd gone. At about two-hundred and forty feet down, her shoulders started to ache and the muscles of her arms burned. She looked up. Already, the cloud-mist had closed in above her. The sun shone only dimly and fuzzily. She was suspended in a gray vaporous emptiness, the only things solid and tangible were her rope and the rock face she walked down. As she climbed lower, the sun grew weaker and the fog thicker.

About halfway to the bottom, her feet found a ledge. She rested there gratefully, allowing her trembling muscles to gather strength. The wind had died down to gentle gusts that cooled the sweat on her face. She looked down. "Is that a glimmer of light down there from my backpack?" she asked herself. "Or are my eyes playing tricks on me?" Her habit of talking to herself, which had never really left her, came back strong now that she was alone again.

"Only one way to tell," she answered.

With a sigh, she stepped off the ledge and continued her climb.

Her eyes weren't playing tricks. As she neared the bottom, she saw the glow of the light stick clearly.

Finally, a foot touched bottom!

When she planted both feet on the ground, they sank in a little, as they would in mud. Brieze took a few cautious steps. The ground supported her, but it was definitely *soft*. She hadn't expected that. She bent down and scooped up a handful of the whitish-colored stuff she was walking on. It was like dirt, but much finer and dryer. It flowed like water between her fingers. It was made of fine, glittering grains, like milled wheat or corn. Brieze had no idea what the stuff was. There were no liquid oceans or deserts on Etherium, no beaches, so she had never encountered sand before.

"Liquid dirt," she said to herself. "Fascinating. I should get a sample."

But she would get the sample later, when she wasn't so tired. Sweat soaked her back. Loose strands of hair clung to her sweaty face. Her hands ached. She sat and slumped against the crystalline rock face she'd just climbed down. She allowed herself to just sit and enjoy the fact she'd made it. She let her weak muscles rest. She looked up at the sky. The sun was just the pale white ghost of a sun far above, shining weakly through the heavy fog. It gave only a little glimmer of light to the world beneath the clouds. When she looked outward, there was only thick mist in every direction. In the distance, vague dark shapes loomed. They could be wrecks. Could be boulders. Could be almost anything. No one had explored this world before. No humans, anyway.

After a half hour's rest she stood up with a groan, brushed herself off, and got to work. She unpacked and pitched her tent, staking it down as best she could in the strange ground. The stakes didn't hold well, so she found heavy rocks to hold down the tent corners. She untied her bundle of firewood and sack of dried meat from her pack. With tinder and flint and a bit of kindling, she lit a small fire—just a few pieces of wood that crackled with yellow flame. She didn't want a large fire. She didn't need one for warmth. It was much warmer beneath the clouds than above them, as she'd known it would be. She wanted a low, slow, steady fire. Bright enough to be seen—and smelled from far away by sensitive noses—but not so large that it appeared strange or threatening.

She unbuttoned her jacket and fished around in the inner pockets of her flightsuit. The suit had many little secret pockets, and despite her excellent memory she sometimes forgot what she had in which of them. Finally, she found what she was looking for. A silver medallion. The silver had been wrought into the shape of two strange-looking hands, empty and palms up. She pinned the medallion to the front of her jacket. She dug into the sack of dried meat and flung a few handfuls of salted goat strips out into the darkness beyond the light of the fire. From her backpack, she pulled out a notebook. She sat by the fire and set it on the ground within easy reach.

She ate a little food and drank a little water. She rested with her back against the rock. The fire spit and popped. It made a pool of light and warmth that stretched only a few yards into the darkness and fog.

Now there was nothing to do but wait. They would come. Sooner or later.

"I hope…" she said.

* * *

Brieze woke with a start. Her fire had burned down to a few red guttering tongues of flame. The sun had disappeared. It was nighttime, and the darkness closed in around her. She sat in a tiny pool of reddish firelight. She couldn't see anything beyond it. Sand slithered and hissed as the wind pushed it about.

She wasn't alone.

Something moved in the darkness. She heard scrabbling sounds and the faint clink of metal on metal. Sniffing. Lips smacking and chewing. Satisfied grunts. Something was eating the goat strips she'd scattered in the dark. Slowly and cautiously, Brieze placed a few more sticks on the fire. It sprang up with crackling yellow flames. She saw the gleam of their eyes as they drew closer to the fire. Big, bulbous eyes, spaced far apart and glimmering green with the light reflecting off their retinas. There were two pairs of eyes and, strangely, a single eye bobbing and blinking all by itself.

But they were Gublins. She'd found them. Her plan had worked so far.

She stood up and shook the sand out of her clothes. "I am a Gublin friend," she said loudly and clearly, and as well as she could, in the Gublin language. "I seek your help."

The eyes blinked and hesitated. The creatures whispered to each other. She couldn't be sure they'd understood her. She could understand the Gublin language well enough, but it was extremely difficult to speak, consisting as it did of variously pitched hisses, punctuated by clicks of the tongue and gurgling sounds made in the back of the throat.

She pointed to the medallion on her jacket, which she was sure they could see. Gublins have excellent eyesight—at least in the dark. She held her empty hands out together, palms up, imitating the gesture of peace the medallion depicted. "A Gublin king of the West gave me this, as a symbol of friendship. It guarantees me safe passage in the Gublin realm."

She wasn't sure how much weight a friendship medallion from a king in the West would carry with these Eastern Gublins, but she figured it was worth something at least. Worth a try, anyway.

They came closer. Vaguely human shapes took form in the fog. When they stepped out of the mist into the firelight, their corpse-white skin took on a faintly bluish glow. Their black eyes fixed on her. These Gublins looked different than the ones she knew—leaner, scruffier, hungrier, and taller, too. Two of them looked to be about six feet tall, and the third one was only a few inches shorter. They were armed, but with only one sword each, not two. They didn't wear armor. Their clothes were made mostly of old spider-silk sailcloth, ingeniously stitched together and interwoven with other cast-off things they'd found—bits of rope and leather and chain. Their hairy ears and thin, colorless lips were pierced with rings and studs of silver and gold. They carried bulky packs on their backs, and the leather straps crisscrossing their chests were strung with all kinds of metal tools, which clinked and clanked together as they moved.

Two of the Gublins hung back behind the first one to emerge from the fog, who seemed to be the leader. He stepped up to Brieze and looked her squarely in the face. He leaned in and sniffed, his nostril slits twitching. Brieze's nose wrinkled. She'd never smelled a Gublin so badly in need of a bath before.

"What *is* it?" One of the ones behind him asked. This one was missing an eye. Where the left one should have been, a round leather patch was sewn right into the skin with black stitches.

"A human," the leader replied, looking Brieze up and down. "A *live* human."

"I've never seen a live one before," the one-eyed one said. "They look funny with flesh on their bones."

"What does it want?" the third, shorter one asked.

The leader locked eyes with Brieze. "What help do you

seek?" he asked.

"I seek the wreck of a ship," she said. "This ship." From her notebook, she took out the blueprints from the construction of the *Atago Maru*, which she had "borrowed" from the naval records. She handed them to the Gublin. He took the blueprint gingerly, almost distrustfully. Gublins don't have paper. They write on sheets of foil. Brieze opened her notebook and tapped a page. "The ship has these markings on the stern. It wrecked here about seventeen years ago."

Without looking up from the blueprint, the Gublin reached out his other hand for the notebook. Gublins are not left-handed or right-handed. They use both equally well and completely independently of each other. Brieze handed him the notebook. He squatted on his lean, stringily-muscled legs and spread the blueprint and the notebook out on the ground in front of him, reading by the light of the fire. The other two Gublins squatted next to him and bent their heads over the paper. They murmured back and forth.

Brieze couldn't get much of what they said. But she knew, from her conversations with Western Gublins, that there was a race of Gublins in the East that scavenged shipwrecks in the Wind's Teeth. Gublins are extremely intelligent and detail oriented. They keep meticulous records, and they share stories. If any Gublins had scavenged the wreck of the *Atago Maru*, she was fairly sure that many of them would know where it was. And she was right. The Gublins that made their living scavenging in the Wind's Teeth knew every wreck along the middle passage as well as a human would know every tree in a favorite park, or every house along their route to the market.

The Gublins finished murmuring. The leader stood up. "We know this ship. If you seek treasure, you will not find it. There is nothing of value left in that ship."

Ah, they knew of it! Wonderful! Brieze's heart flooded with warm relief. "I do not seek treasure," she said. "I seek a book."

"A book...?" The Gublin asked, puzzled.

"Like this one," she pointed to the notebook.

The Gublin shrugged. "It may be there. We would have no need of such a thing. It must be a very valuable...book."

"It is to me," she said. "Will you take me to the wreck?"

"It is three day's walk from here, on the way we are traveling. We could take you." The Gublin paused. "What will you offer us for our help?"

"This!" Brieze said, picking up and hefting the five-pound sack of salted goat strips.

The Gublin's nostril slits quivered. A greedy, ravenous light shone in his eyes. His black pointed tongue snaked out to lick his pale lips and sharp teeth. The other two stood up, the same light shining in their eyes. Brieze had bet right. Gublins everywhere are crazy for goat meat. It's so much better than anything they have to eat in the underworld. On her last visit to a Gublin realm, she had been offered beetles, bats, and a centipede stew. She'd politely refused, of course.

They edged closer. Brieze stood her ground. She'd brought along a knife, which was tucked into her belt. But even so she was, for all practical purposes, completely defenseless. Even a full-grown human trained in combat would

208 • JEFF MINERD

be no match for one Gublin, much less three. They were simply too fast. Then the one-eyed one said something she hadn't expected, something she'd never imagined a Gublin would say, from what she knew of them. Something that left her dizzy and unable to breathe.

"Let's kill it," he said. "Take its meat and anything else it has we can use, and be on our way."

There was a silence for a second or two that became an eternity for Brieze. The leader looked at her as if he were considering, his eyes going to the medallion on her chest.

"No need to kill the silly thing," the shorter one said. "Let's just leave it be."

"Shut up, both of you," the leader said. "A live human could be helpful. It will know many things about their ships that could be useful to us."

"I do," Brieze said in a rush. "I know a lot. Anything you want to know."

"Then we agree," the leader said. "Hurry and pack up your things. We are already behind schedule."

"Wait!" Brieze said, summoning up what she knew of Gublin culture and their codes of ethics. "You have to swear, on the honor of your clan, that you won't harm me. That you'll take me to the wreck as you promised."

There was a pause.

"We swear," the leader said, though without much enthusiasm.

"We swear," the other two echoed. "On the honor of our clan."

"Now let us go, quickly," the leader said.

"Wait!" she said. "I need you to bring me back, too. Back here to this spot. I won't be able to find my way back alone."

The leader made an unpleasant gurgling sound. The other two hissed in distress. They argued among themselves. Finally, the leader turned to Brieze. "My companions cannot take you back. We will lose too much time. However, I myself will bring you back to this spot for…," he moved closer and pointed to the silver medallion, "…that. That might be very valuable to me."

Brieze hated to give up the friendship medallion the Gublin king had given her. She doubted it was meant to be traded at will. And a very large part of her was urging her to call the whole thing off, to scurry back up that rope as fast as she could to the safety of the *Devious* on the ledge above. To fly back to the Palace of Kyo and the family that waited for her there.

But if there was even a chance of finding her father's journal…

"Deal," she said.

✳   ✳   ✳

The three-day walk with a heavy pack on her back was the hardest thing Brieze had done in her life. The three-mile walk from the port of Kyo to Mamma Kasshoku's boarding house was a tea party by comparison. The sand shifted under her feet, slowing her progress and keeping her constantly off balance. At least she had sturdy boots for walking this time. But the damned gritty stuff got into her boots and irritated her fiercely. The wind blew it into her eyes and managed to get it under her clothes, where it itched.

Still, she did her best to keep up and walk beside the leader, whose name was Zeelak. He asked her question after question, which she answered breathlessly as she struggled to match his pace. What type of cargo did merchant ships carry these days? How many warships did her kingdom have? How old were the ships in her fleet? What kinds of metals were used in their construction? She answered as best she could, and when she didn't know an answer she guessed but presented it as truth. She wasn't about to appear ignorant or unhelpful.

She managed to ask Zeelak some questions in return. Did he know how the Wind's Teeth had been formed? How about the liquid dirt? How many wrecks were down here? How many had he scavenged? He answered her tersely. Nobody knew how the Teeth had formed, although some Gublins thought they were made of a kind of crystal that was somehow able to grow. The "liquid dirt," as she called it, was created as wind, rain, and lighting strikes eroded the Teeth. Nobody knew how many wrecks were down here. He had scavenged fifty-two so far in his life.

The other two Gublins, Zeetog and Zeefor, didn't talk to her at all. But they complained about her to Zeelak as they marched. They did this right in front of her, as if she weren't even there, referring to her as "it" or "the human."

"The human is slow," Zeefor, the one-eyed one, said. "It is making us late."

"It talks too much," said the shorter one, Zeetog. "Its voice is annoying, like a whining baby's."

"Shut up you two," said Zeelak, "or I'll make one of you carry her."

"I'd be happy to carry the human…," Zeefor said. "In my belly!" He snickered. "It eats such tasty meat, it must be delicious itself."

"Shut up!" Zeelak said. "Keep moving."

Zeefor edged up behind Brieze. He whispered softy in her ear, so only she heard. "Beware, tasty human. I often wake up in the middle of the night. Hungry for a snack." He chortled.

Brieze's heart thudded even faster than it had already been thudding. She was pretty sure that Zeefor swearing on the honor of his clan prevented him from eating her in the middle of the night. Still, she hunched her shoulders as she trudged and tried to make herself look as small and unappetizing as possible. She didn't ask Zeelak any more questions.

✳ ✳ ✳

The feeble sun came up as they walked through a barren, mist-shrouded landscape, following a narrow valley that snaked its way through the roots of the Teeth, heading south toward the middle passage. The Teeth themselves rose to dizzying heights all around them, losing themselves in the fog above. Brieze counted her paces and noted their direction, filing the information away in her memory, just in case she needed it to return. There was no knowing what might happen on this journey, and if she found herself alone at least she'd have a rough map in her mind of how to get back to her starting point. It would give her a chance, at least.

At midday, with the pale sun glimmering in the haze directly above them, they came to the middle passage. The slippery, shifting ground sloped down to a wider valley, running east-west. The desolate valley was filled with sand, which the wind had shaped into row upon row of rippling dunes. They stretched off into the distance. Brieze had never seen anything like this. The wind gusted stronger here. The sand stung her face. It began to snow—fat, wet flakes that whirled and mixed with the airborne grit. They climbed down into the valley, then headed west, plodding up and down each treacherous dune.

They came upon the hulking wreck of a ship that loomed out of the fog—very old, half buried. The ribs of its hull poked up out of the sand. Between its ribs, the planks of its upper and lower decks had collapsed into a jumbled pile. Its masts had toppled like sickly trees. Brieze wanted to stop to investigate, but Zeelak refused, urging them on. "It's an old wreck, nothing interesting there," he said. "You'll see many more like that before we reach the ship you want."

"I just want to see what kind of ship it is," Brieze said.

"It's a *crashed* ship. Anyone can see that," Zeelak said, not slowing his stride. "Foolish humans flying around in such dangerous contraptions, made of such flimsy material. It's a wonder you haven't all died and gone extinct." Gublins, who make most everything they need from stone or metal, have nothing but contempt for wood. In their opinion, the fragile, splintery stuff is completely unsuitable for making anything. They don't even use it for fuel, finding coal to be far superior.

Not far from the wreck, they came upon the remains of three airmen. They sat huddled together, back to back, buried to their waists. They were nothing but bones and a few flapping, tattered remains of cloth. Their skulls nodded, staring down into their laps. Their ribs interlaced as they slowly crumbled into one another. Brieze wanted to stop to investigate these too, but Zeelak again refused. "You'll see many more of those, too," he said. "One dead human is much like another."

When the sun set, Zeelak called a halt and they made camp. The Gublins dropped their packs with a groan and had a meal. Zeelak rationed the goat meat among them. Zeetog and Zeefor ate with smacking lips, then complained they didn't get enough. "Don't be so stingy," Zeefor said. "Give us more!"

"Fools," Zeelak replied. "The two of you would eat the entire bag in one sitting, then not be able to walk because of your swollen, cramping bellies."

"But I'm still *hungry*," Zeefor complained, fixing his one eye on Brieze and licking his lips.

She made herself eat some bread and dried fruit, swallowed down with water and a fair amount of sand. She had enough food and water to last about a week. More if she stretched it, which she probably would. She didn't have much of an appetite.

The Gublins didn't erect any kind of shelter. They

wormed themselves into the sand and slept there with their heads on their packs. They seemed perfectly comfortable in the nasty environment. Brieze struggled for a long while to pitch her tent. The stakes wouldn't stay in the ground at all, and she couldn't find any good rocks to weigh down the corners. The wind kept trying to yank the uncooperative tangle of poles and fabric out of her hands. Once, the tent caught a good gust and nearly dragged her along the ground. She was reminded of a passage in a history book that suggested the principle of air travel was discovered by some ancient person trying to hold down a tent on a windy day. As she cursed and fought a losing battle against the wind, she saw how that was possible. In the end, she gave up, rolled up the tent and stuffed it back in her pack. She wrapped herself in a blanket, wormed herself into the sand like the Gublins, and slept fitfully.

Some instinct woke her in the middle of the night. Everything was black save for the vaguest fuzzy hint of a moon, low in the sky. But something nearby caught and reflected that suggestion of moonlight. A single eye, gleaming in the dark. Low to the ground, it was inching toward her. She heard ragged breathing and indistinct muttering. Smacking lips. She was too afraid to move, but she made herself move anyway. Silently, she rummaged through her pack until her blind fingers found what they were searching for. They closed around a cool glass cylinder. She pulled the light stick from her pack and shook it hard.

The glass rod blazed with blue white light.

Zeefor, crouching not ten feet from her, leapt up with a

shriek and clamped both his hands over his one good eye. To a Gublin eye, that kind of light hurt like a dagger.

His shriek woke Zeelak and Zeetog. They covered their eyes too, and cursed the light.

"Put that thing away!" Zeelak shouted. "What's going on here?"

Brieze doused the light by stuffing the rod inside her jacket. Still, some of the glow leaked and shone through, making her look like some kind of ghost, or sorcerer, in the night.

"He was sneaking up on me!" She shouted. "He was going to eat me...or something!"

Zeefor recovered some of his composure. He pointed a long bony finger at her accusingly. "I only got up in the night to relieve myself, and the stupid human attacked me with that awful thing."

"Settle down, both of you," Zeelak said. "And get back to sleep. We rise in a few hours."

Zeefor shuffled away, mumbling, and wriggled himself back into the sand.

The glow from the light stick faded. But Brieze spent the rest of the night gripping it in a sweaty hand, her ears straining to catch any suspicious noises.

* * *

The next day they came across an unusual sight. It was one of the Wind's Teeth, but a tiny one, standing in the valley of the middle passage apart from the others. It was no more than a hundred feet high and maybe thirty feet in diameter. They had encountered a few of these small teeth poking up out of the sand before. But this one was unusual because its top had been blasted off by a lightning strike. Molten bits of it had dribbled down its side like hardened candle wax. And brittle pieces of it were strewn everywhere—chunks the size of boulders, and shards like glittering blades poking up out of the sand.

"This is new," Zeetog said. "This happened since we last came this way."

"Be very careful where you step," Zeelak said.

But he'd no sooner said this when Zeefor shrieked in pain, hopped about on one foot, then crumpled to a sitting position, clutching his other foot. They all ran over to see what was the matter. Zeefor had stepped on one of the bladelike shards. Gublins don't wear shoes. The stone had sliced deeply into the leathery sole of his webbed foot. Black Gublin blood sluiced out of the wound, dripping onto the sand.

"Quickly, bind it up! Stanch the blood!" Zeelak yelled.

"We are doomed!" Zeetog moaned.

"Curse my clumsiness!" Zeefor said with a grimace.

"It's not that bad of a wound," Brieze said. "I could sew it up with some needle and thread."

"Ignorant human," Zeelak glared at her. "The scent of blood could wake the Sleepers. They smell it from miles away."

"The Sleepers?" she asked.

"We must all get to higher ground. Hurry!"

Zeelak hastily bound Zeefor's foot with a rag, then hauled him to his feet. He ordered the group to run as fast as they could to the small tooth with the blasted-off top and to scale it. The Gublins took off at a Gublin-fast pace, kicking up spouts of sand and leaving Brieze far behind as she ran uncertainly after them. "What's going on?" she called, out of breath.

"Run, human, *run!*" Zeelak shouted over his shoulder.

By the time Brieze reached the base of the tooth, her heart pounding, the Gublins had already scaled it and were looking down at her, urging her to climb. Gublins can climb anything made of stone as easily as most humans can walk up a flight of stairs. She looked up at the vertical rock face above her and saw very little in the way of hand- or foot-holds that would support her. She made a half-hearted attempt at a climb, then dropped back down to the ground after scaling only a few feet.

"Why are we doing this?" she called to them. "I don't see what the problem is."

"Look!" Zeelak shouted, pointing out into the valley.

She looked, and saw something strange. Out in the distance—it was hard to tell exactly how far in the foggy, featureless landscape—the sand was seething and rippling as if something were moving just underneath the surface.

Moving toward her. Fast.

She made a real effort to climb this time, clawing at the rock, forgetting to make sure her footing was firm and to use her legs to push herself up. She lost her grip and fell, cutting up her knees and chin as she slid down. She hit the ground feet first and fell onto her back. She struggled to right herself. Her heavy pack held her down. She heard the sound of an immense slithering through the sand, growing louder.

"The weak human can't climb!" Zeetog shouted.

"Leave it for the Sleepers," Zeefor said. "If it satisfies them, we can save ourselves!"

But Zeelak had already uncoiled one of the long, sturdy lengths of rope they carried. "We have offered her our service. She is bound to us. Help me bring her up." He tossed the rope down to Brieze, who'd managed to get back onto her feet. She grabbed the rope and hastily tied it around her waist. She gripped it tightly with both hands. She felt something—some *things* actually—worming their way up her legs. The Gublins pulled, and her feet lifted off the ground. Gublins are not just faster than humans, they are stronger too, despite their spindly appearance. Three of them pulling on the rope hand-over-hand yanked Brieze to the top in a matter of seconds.

As they lifted her over the edge and deposited her on the wide, flat summit, she felt something biting at her legs, right through the sturdy fabric of her trousers. There were *things* crawling on her! She yelped and slapped at her legs until they were all dead. There were half-a-dozen of them; the vanguard of a much larger group. She picked up one of their crumpled, twitching bodies between a thumb and forefinger and studied it.

It was a fat black worm-like thing, a couple of inches long. Segmented like a centipede but without any legs. Its tapered body appeared to slither through the sand. It clung to her fingers with fine, prickly hairs. Serrated, scissor-like mandibles stuck out from its head. Brieze's legs were on fire where they had bitten her. She flicked the thing over the edge.

"What are they?" she asked. "I didn't think anything lived down here."

"The Sleepers do," Zeelak said. "They can lie dormant for years, even decades, until they smell blood. Then they awaken, and won't sleep again until they have eaten."

"Can they climb up here?"

"No. They do not leave the sand."

"So, we're safe now?" Brieze shrugged off her pack. The flat summit seemed spacious enough for them to stay there comfortably. "We can wait up here until they go away?"

"No," Zeelak said. "They won't go away. One of us must die."

* * *

As Zeelak stitched up Zeefor's foot with a needle and thread, he explained the situation to Brieze.

The Sleepers lived in huge colonies made up of thousands and thousands of individuals. They were intelligent, seeming to share one group mind, and they acted as one organism. They would have followed Zeefor's blood trail. They knew their prey was trapped atop the tooth. Already, they would have surrounded its base.

Brieze looked out over the edge. The sand below burbled and rippled.

Now, the Sleepers would wait, Zeelak explained. They could wait a long time. Long after the four of them starved to death atop the tooth and their flesh had turned to dust, the Sleepers would still be waiting. The creatures might go dormant, or semi-dormant, but their senses would be heightened, sharply focused around the base of the tooth. If anyone tried to climb down and escape by foot, they would be attacked the moment they touched the ground. The Sleepers' countless, tiny, ravenous jaws could strip a full-grown Gublin down to the bone in a matter of minutes.

"They will only truly sleep again if they feed," Zeelak said. "Therefore, we must play the game."

"The game?" she asked.

"We will draw lots to see which one of us will be sacrificed to the Sleepers so the others may live."

"Well I'm not playing any such ga—"

Three Gublin swords sang free of their sheaths and pointed at her throat before she finished the thought. She blinked, stunned by the sheer speed of it. She'd seen Gublin swordplay before, but she'd forgotten how inhumanly *fast* they really were.

"You are bound to us," Zeelak said. "The rules are very clear. You will play the game, or *you* will be the one we feed to the Sleepers."

Brieze nodded. She couldn't think of any other response with those swords pointing at her.

The Gublins sheathed their swords. Zeelak produced a leather drawstring bag and four small, round, polished stones—three white and one black. The Gublins used such stones for many of the games they played, most of them more pleasant than this one. He showed the stones to all of them, placed the stones in the bag, and shook it. "Now we choose," he said.

Gublins have strict rules about rank and seniority. The rules required Zeelak to choose first. Then Zeetog, Zeefor, and finally Brieze, who was the lowliest member of the group. Zeelak reached into the bag. He had a three out of four chance of drawing a white stone. He did.

"Now Zeetog," Zeelak held the bag out to him. Zeetog reached in. He had a two out of three chance of drawing a white stone. He did. But he didn't smile at his good luck. He looked anxiously at Zeefor, who was his cousin and friend.

"Now Zeefor," Zeelak held out the bag. Zeefor reached in. He had a fifty-fifty chance of drawing a white stone. The outcome of the game would be decided by his draw. Whatever stone he got, Brieze's stone would be the opposite. She wouldn't need to draw herself.

It was not Zeefor's lucky day. He drew the black stone.

He stared at it for a while, rolling it between his fingers, his lips twitching. Then he hurled the stone away with a snarl and backed away from the others, putting a hand on the hilt of his sword. "I won't be sacrificed when we have a perfectly good live human here that will do the trick!" he said.

Zeelak put his hand on the hilt of his sword. "The rules are very clear," he said. "You played the game. You drew the black stone."

"You'd sacrifice *me*, one of your own *clan,* instead of this human?"

"You are shaming yourself and dishonoring us all," Zeelak said. "Gather up your courage and do what needs to be done."

Zeefor drew his sword. "You want my life? Come get it if you can."

Zeelak drew his sword. "You sadden me, cousin."

They crouched into fighting stances.

"Wait!" Brieze said, finding her voice. "There has to be a better way."

Zeelak spoke through clenched teeth. "Unless you can conjure up one of your airships and fly us far away from here, silly human, this is the only way."

The thought smacked her in the center of her forehead.

"Wait!" she said, "I can *do* that. I can do *exactly* that!"

SEVENTEEN

It was a cold and clear-skied morning when Tak and Jon approached the Wind's Teeth. They gleamed in the light of the newly risen sun like something out of a dream, left over from the night before. Their sharp peaks rose so impossibly high into the sky, it looked as if they reached the pale crescent moon that hung above them. Their crystalline flanks sparkled. They managed to look utterly beautiful, quietly menacing, and not-quite-real all at the same time. They reminded the boys that they were very far from home, in a part of the world that was wonderful and wild, and definitely dangerous.

Tak whistled in awe. "*Look* at 'em," he said. "They *can't* be that big. They make the Highspire Mountains look like dunghills. I mean, just *look* at 'em."

Jon was looking—with wide eyes. He stood in the bow of the *Arrow*, gripping the foremast tightly with one hand, as if he were afraid the Teeth might somehow snatch him right off the deck. He was in all likelihood the only living person from Pinemont ever to see the Wind's Teeth. The lumberjacks of Pinemont were not voyagers. The farthest any of them usually journeyed was the two-day trip across the Ocean of Clouds to the Dragonback Mountains, to log the pine forests there. But they told stories about the Teeth on Pinemont. Stories about monsters that lurked within them. Stories of malevolent winds that played deadly tricks. Jon was a brave boy, even recklessly so. He'd happily take on ten men with his axe if the need arose. But his courage vanished completely in the face of the Teeth.

Tak close-hauled the *Arrow's* sail so the ship drifted slowly on the current. The winter chill reddened his cheeks and nose. A light snow fell, catching in his hair, which had grown back to its usual shaggy state. He pulled his cloak more tightly around himself and sat on one of the thwart benches. He opened his father's logbook and unfolded the map. Tak senior had gone through the Teeth with a convoy of merchant ships. He had marked the entrance to the middle passage on the chart, noting its precise latitude and longitude. Of their passage through the Teeth, he wrote: *Entering them was like leaving this world entirely. The wind was rough, and constantly changing direction, but other than that we had no trouble. Captain Ekstrom is a veteran of many passages. I swear he can smell the wind changing.*

Jon sat on the bench across from Tak, facing him.

He cleared his throat.

"Why haven't we turned north," he asked. "To go around them?"

Tak didn't answer. He sat hunched over the map, tracing a route with his finger. He felt a strange sense of satisfaction at being the quiet one for a change. He said nothing because he could see Jon was afraid of the Teeth, and he knew the things he was about to say would make him very unhappy.

Jon tried again, as if he could get the answer he wanted to hear—desperately needed to hear—by asking a different question. "How long will it take," he growled, "to go *around* them?"

"It would take two weeks," Tak said. "If we flew around them."

That *if* hit Jon like a punch to the gut. It made his legs go weak and shaky. "If…?" he gasped. "If…?"

"It'll take one *day* to go through," Tak said.

"I'd rather get there two weeks later than not at all."

Tak held up the logbook. "My father's convoy made it through without a hitch. His notes say it was incredible. Most ships pass through without a problem."

"Key word there is *most*," Jon crossed his arms. "Why risk it if we don't have to?"

Tak realized that he and Jon were having a conversation. An actual back-and-forth conversation. Fear had loosened Jon's tongue. Tak wished it could be happening under better circumstances. And he knew it would end soon, because he had a trick that would make Jon agree, but it was a low dirty trick. Tak knew he would hate himself for it, and Jon would hate him too.

"Are you scared?" Tak asked. "If you're too scared, just say so and we'll go around."

Jon clenched his jaw and fumed. Admitting to fear was simply not allowed among boys and young men in the King-dom of Spire. It was an unwritten rule, but a powerful one, drilled-in at an early age. Jon wanted to do it, the words were right there at his lips, but he couldn't. Instead, he snorted like a rhinoceros and spit a huge gob of phlegm over the side. He would have like to spit it in Tak's face. His expression made that abundantly clear.

"Screw you," he said. "Do what you want. I don't care."

Tak felt awful. But the ploy worked.

* * *

Flying through the Wind's Teeth in the *Arrow* made Tak feel like a gnat gliding through a dense forest of bizarre, white-trunked trees. Once they were far enough inside that the Teeth appeared to close in behind them, the wind became eerily calm. But Tak heard it all around them— moaning and muttering, whispering and snickering. He gripped the tiller with a sweaty hand, and his feet squirmed on the wing flap pedals. He checked his lifeline. Jon checked both of his lifelines—he had attached not one but *two* to his belt. Then he resumed his two-armed death grip on the aft mast. He faced forward so that Tak, who was sitting in the stern, couldn't see he was squeezing his eyes tightly shut.

They hit a pocket of turbulence—a hole in the wind that dropped them twenty feet like a stone before the air caught them again. Tak lifted off his seat, then came down on it hard, jarring his teeth. Jon's feet left the deck. He made a strangled sound in the back of his throat. He lost his grip on the mast and tumbled to the deck. The *Arrow* bounced and rocked, its sail flapping in agitation.

"Are you all right?" Tak asked.

Jon didn't answer right away. Instead, he crawled on his hands and knees to a storage compartment and fished out a coil of rope. He used it to lash himself to the aft mast, winding it in tight turns around his body again and again, from his knees to under his arms. He tied the rope off with a sturdy woodsman's knot.

"Don't talk to me," he said, clamping his eyes shut again. "Tell me when it's over."

Tak was about to try to say something encouraging or comforting to Jon when his attention was diverted—he saw something that couldn't possibly be real.

His father, Taktinius Spinner senior, stood in the bow of the *Arrow*, facing him. He wore a sweat-soaked nightshirt that hung to his knees. His hair was matted and sweaty, his eyes red-rimmed and wild-looking. Neither his nightshirt nor his hair stirred in the wind as they should have. His father looked as surprised and mystified to see Tak as Tak was to see him. Tak senior looked around, and realized where they were, in the Wind's Teeth. He looked back at Tak and shook his head in warning. He waved his arms and said something that Tak couldn't hear. But the message was clear—*go back*!

Tak blinked and shook his head, and the vision was gone.

At that moment, the *Arrow*'s sail luffed and chattered.

Tak felt the pressure drop in his ears. He heard the approaching roar.

The wind attacked them.

A rogue current hit them head-on with gale force. A wall of wind lifted the bow of the *Arrow* and turned the ship completely upside down, tumbling it end-over-end. Tak was hurled from his seat in the stern out into the sky—but his lifeline held. It yanked on his belt so hard the breath was squeezed out of him. He and the *Arrow* whirled around and around, connected by the slim tether. Things were happening so fast, he couldn't make sense of what he was seeing. He caught flashes of things—ropes whipping back and forth, the sail tearing away from its yard, Jon still tied to the mast, his red hair flying. Jon was screaming a scream that started deep and throaty, but rose to a shrill squeaky shriek.

The wind played with them the way a cat plays with a mouse, batting them this way and that. But all the while the current carried them back the way they came. It carried them right to the edge of the Teeth and spit them out the way they'd come in. Once free of the Teeth, the current spent itself and the *Arrow* stopped tumbling. It ended up completely capsized, upside down. Tak dangled from his lifeline below his ship, nothing beneath his feet but empty sky and the clouds that blanketed Etherium's surface far, far below.

He looked up.

Jon was there, not far above him. Still tied tightly to the aft mast. Upside down. His shaggy red hair dangled in the wind. His eyes were open now. His arms were crossed, and he was glowering at Tak. Glowering hard and accusingly.

He channeled a *lot* of anger into that look.

"Okay, *okay*," Tak said. "We'll go around."

✳   ✳   ✳

Tak righted the *Arrow* without too much difficulty. He'd done it many times before. It was a matter of climbing up the lifeline hand over hand, standing on the underside of one of the wings, gripping the keel, and leaning and rocking until the ship flipped over right side up. Tak helped Jon untie himself. Jon did not thank him for the help. He went immediately to the side storage compartment where his axe had been stowed to retrieve it, letting out a relieved sigh when he found it still there, cradling it in his arms. Tak frowned. He was hoping the axe might have gotten loose, as it always seemed to do, and fallen out of the ship. No such luck.

The boys looked over the ship for damage. They didn't find anything too serious. The sail had torn in places, a few lines and stays had snapped; nothing that couldn't be fixed in short order with the tools they had on hand.

Except for one very important thing.

The water casks.

All but one of them was gone.

The casks on the deck of the *Arrow* had been lashed tightly to the gunwales, the sturdy ropes run through brackets mounted there. When Tak tied up the casks, he'd only thought about keeping them from getting loose and sliding or rolling around the deck. He hadn't considered the possibility the ship might be turned upside-down and tossed around by a malicious wind. When that happened, all but one of the heavy, five-gallon casks had wiggled free of their bonds. They were long gone. The loops of rope that had held them lay slack upon the deck.

The boys made some quick calculations. If they went on half-rations of water, two quarts a day, they had enough to last ten days. If they went on quarter rations, they could stretch that to twenty days possibly. The problem was, they were smack dab in the middle of nowhere. The Eastern Kingdoms were more than a month away, and it would take the same amount of time to get back home. They'd be without water for at least ten days, and the longest a person could survive without water was three. Four tops.

"That's it," Jon said, leaning on his axe. "We're dead. We're gonna die of thirst."

Tak sat with his father's navigational chart on his knees, studying it desperately. After a few moments, he announced, "There is one place we can reach in time."

"Where?" Jon asked, peering at the map.

Tak pointed to it with a finger. "No-Man's Crag," he said.

An unhappy silence fell upon them. They had heard of the Crag. The small, misshapen mountain poked its ugly head above the surface clouds within sight of the northern Teeth. No-Man's Crag had only one town upon it, Port Roil. It was a pirate town, rowdy and lawless, home to a loosely knit band of thieves and outlaws that called themselves the Brotherhood. The Crag was far enough away from any lawful kingdom that none of them bothered with it. It was close to the Wind's Teeth, which was ideal for pirates, and it was just a short voyage away from the Dragonlord's realm, which was convenient, as pirates sold their captives as slaves to the Dragonlord.

Jon sat on the gunwale with a defeated sigh, his axe on his knees, his head in his hands. He hadn't yet recovered his courage, and he'd had enough of this journey. He was sorry he'd ever decided to come along. The cramped quarters and lousy food. The constant talking. Nearly being killed in The Wind's Teeth. And now they were going to try and get water from pirates.

"They'll rob us," he said. "Beat us. Sell us as slaves."

"Maybe not," Tak shrugged. "And if they do, they'll at least have to give us water and keep us alive."

No-Man's Crag wouldn't be hard to find. Tak's father had circled it in bright red ink, and jotted down its latitude and longitude. Underneath this, in bold red letters, he had written STEER CLEAR.

EIGHTEEN

The key to Brieze's plan was her tent. With its canvas and wooden poles, she could construct a two-seated glider, the kind of simple flying device every young child in the Kingdom of Spire enjoyed taking to the park on a windy day. It would basically be just one large wing, she explained to the Gublins, with a seat suspended beneath it. The steering would be rudimentary, and it could only carry two at a time, but it would suffice if she flew each Gublin to a safe distance individually, making three trips.

Gublins aren't afraid of heights, as long as they are touching stone. During the siege of Selestria, they climbed the hundred-foot-high walls of Castle Selestria, perched at the very top of Selemont. But Gublins, who live mainly underground, do not fly. The thought of flying, of losing all contact with the earth and trusting oneself to the whims of the wind, fills them with a queasy dread. None of the three Gublins—not even Zeefor—looked enthused about the plan. But they discussed it, and agreed it was worth a try.

If you need to turn a tent into a glider in a hurry, the help of three Gublins comes in extremely handy. They are good at making things. Their long, nimble fingers can tie knots that would amaze and baffle the most experienced airmen. They are skilled in the making and use of tools. These Gublins had plenty of tools, and needle and thread, including spider-silk thread they'd scavenged from ships, which was stronger than steel. They also had a tin of a very suitable fast-acting adhesive. Brieze made a few sketches of the glider in her notebook. The Gublins studied these, talked among themselves, asked her many questions, then went to work. She supervised, ordering tweaks and changes as necessary. The position and balance of the seat was especially important.

In a short time, they'd fashioned a glider that looked much stronger and more airworthy than Brieze had expected. The rectangular canvas wing, framed with wooden poles, was eight feet long from tip to tip. The U-shaped, saddle-like seat was attached to the wing with ropes in the front and back. Once the glider was finished, the Gublins had to hold onto it tightly, as the wind was already trying to pull it up into the sky.

"Nice work," Brieze said. "I think I could fly this back to Kyo if I had to."

"A half-mile will suffice," Zeelak said. "Can this flimsy thing really carry us that far?"

"I don't see why not. Let me take if for a test run."

She directed the Gublins to take hold of each end of the wing and raise it as far above their heads as possible. She stood in front of the seat and gripped the ropes. She took a running start and leapt out into the sky, pulling the glider along with her.

The glider dipped on takeoff, but caught the wind and soared. The wood and canvas creaked. Brieze lowered herself into the seat. She grinned at the weightless free feeling, at the wind rushing past her face. She couldn't help it. It had been too long since she'd been in the sky. The balance of the seat was good. She tested the steering, first pulling on the rear ropes to angle the wing upward. The glider rose. She pulled on the front ropes to angle the wing downward. The glider dove. She pulled and leaned left, and the glider turned left. She pulled and leaned right, and it turned right. She made a long curving right turn, steering the glider back to the small tooth, which was already hard to see in the fog.

She returned to the summit, flying into the wind and angling the wing sharply upward to execute a stall landing that dropped her neatly among the amazed Gublins. Tak would have been proud, she thought, and it made her heart twinge. She hadn't thought of him in forever. She felt guilty about that. What was he doing now? What would he think of her, hunting for a shipwreck in the roots of the Wind's Teeth with three Gublins? He wouldn't like it. He would want to be with her. Best not to think of him now, she supposed. Concentrate on the matter at hand.

The Gublin rules required that Brieze fly Zeelak to safety first, then Zeetog, and finally Zeefor. She didn't like this, and she explained why. It meant that she and Zeefor would have to launch the glider by themselves, without any assistance. That was much more difficult and dangerous. And Zeefor had a bad foot, which would make the launch even more of a problem.

"Zeefor and I should go first," she said to Zeelak, "with you and Zeetog assisting the launch."

"Yes!" Zeefor agreed. "I should go first. Because of my bad foot."

"You are lucky to be going at all," Zeelak said. "I should have killed you for your dishonorable behavior. I will go first, as the rules dictate. Let us begin."

Brieze directed Zeelak to stand next to her, in front of the glider seat, while the other two Gublins held the wing high over their heads. He took hold of the right-hand ropes, she took hold of the left. He gritted his teeth. They ran and leapt into the sky. He closed his eyes and gurgled as the glider dipped. He was no happier when it caught the wind and soared. But Gublins are nimble, and agile. He lowered himself into the seat without making the glider rock.

"You did that well," she said.

Zeelak didn't open his eyes. "Get us to safety before I soil myself."

She flew as far away as she could, about a half-mile, until she could just barely make out the reddish glow of the small fire they had built atop the tooth so she could find her way back through the fog. She leaned and pulled on the ropes. The glider swooped low to the ground. "Jump!" she said, and Zeelak—opening his eyes and seeing solid ground not far below him—eagerly did so. He slid off the seat and hit the ground rolling. The glider, free of his weight, rose on the wind.

"I'll be back soon with Zeetog," she called, steering the

glider on a return course.

The trip with Zeetog was more difficult. There was only Zeefor to assist with holding the wing aloft, so the launch was clumsier. Zeetog shrieked as his feet left the ground. He squeezed his eyes shut and babbled to himself the entire trip. He didn't notice when they reached the spot where Zeelak waited below. He didn't hear Brieze's order to jump. She had to push him off. He shrieked again and curled up into a ball. He didn't appear to suffer any damage when he hit the sand, though.

Brieze returned to the tooth where Zeefor waited.

She hadn't thought about the fact she'd be alone with him. She didn't like the way he looked at her with that one glistening, filmy black eye. She sensed unhealthy thoughts festering behind it. His long, bony fingers clenched and un-clenched.

"Come on," she said. "Stand here next to me and take a hold of those ropes. And help me hold the wing aloft with your other hand."

He limped over on his bad, bandaged foot and stood next to her, but he only half-heartedly did as she instructed. The wind had grown stronger, and it tugged hard at the glider wing. Brieze struggled to keep it steady and in the right posi-tion. Zeefor was little help. He was having second thoughts about this plan—especially after seeing Zeetog take off shrieking and disappear into the sky. He twitched and grim-aced and muttered to himself.

"We should have fed you to the Sleepers," he said. "Then I wouldn't have to fly in this awful thing."

"Let's just get it over with," she said. "You'll be back on the ground in minutes."

"Wait a moment," he said. "I forgot something. I'll be right back."

He limped away and left her standing there struggling to control the glider by herself. She turned to look over her shoulder. He was right behind her, rummaging through the bits of equipment they had left behind to lighten their packs. But she couldn't keep her eyes on him. She had to pay attention to the glider.

"Hurry up," she called over her shoulder. "I can't hold this thing by myself."

And then she sensed him rushing up behind her—heard the quick flapping of his feet and a hiss of pain. Her back felt exposed and vulnerable. Instinctively, she jumped away with the glider, off the edge…

He lunged at her with a short knife. A knife he'd planned to stick into her back. If he hadn't been slowed by his injured foot, he would have stabbed her and thrown her over the edge before she even knew what was happening. "I *won't* fly. I'll feed you to the Sleepers!" he screeched, slashing at her legs as the glider lifted her up and away on the wind. She kicked at him. The tip of his knife stuck in her boot heel.

Not deep enough to cut her.

Just deep enough to yank Zeefor off-balance as she swung her foot.

He let go of the knife, flailed his arms to try to get his balance back, and toppled over the edge.

He screamed as he fell.

The glider rocked and yawed, wildly off balance. Brieze had landed sideways on the seat during the panicked launch. One of her legs was tangled up in the ropes. There was no way to control the glider. It was dropping fast. She grabbed at one of the ropes above her head and pulled on it as hard as she could, angling the wing upward to try to get some lift. But she only delayed the crash by a few seconds. She and the glider hit the sand with the sounds of splintering wood and ripping canvas and rolled several yards. She disentangled herself from the wreckage as fast as she could, took Zeefor's knife out of her boot heel, and jumped to her feet. She was maybe a hundred yards away from the small tooth. At a spot near its base, the ground boiled like water. Something thrashed there, splashing sand in every direction. She couldn't see Zeefor. But, faintly, she heard his screams.

She turned and ran as fast as she could, her pack bouncing furiously up and down on her shoulders. She ran blindly into the fog until she couldn't run anymore, couldn't breathe anymore. She dropped to the ground, gasping for air, and prayed she was far enough away from the Sleepers. She lay there for several minutes. The minutes became half an hour. She got her breath back. Nothing swam through the sand to devour her. Finally, she stood up with a groan. She took a light stick from her backpack, shook it, and stumbled around in the fog, calling out for Zeelak and Zeetog.

The Gublins found her a few hours later. It was their keen noses that drew them in the right direction, until they could see her light and hear her voice.

"Put that light away!" Zeelak ordered, squinting and

shielding his eyes.

"Where is Zeefor?" Zeetog asked in a panicked voice.

Brieze took a breath and told them what happened. As proof, she showed them Zeefor's knife, and the hole it had made in her boot heel. She handed the knife to Zeelak. Zeetog's lips quivered. She had never seen a Gublin cry before. She didn't know they could cry. Zeetog sat down on the sand and put his head in his heads. He burbled like a child. His shoulders shook. Fat, shiny tears slid down his face.

Zeelak's face was hard and expressionless as he turned the knife over and over in his hands.

"He drew the black stone," was all he said.

✶   ✶   ✶

"There is the ship you seek," Zeelak pointed ahead into the fog.

At first, Brieze didn't see anything. But as they walked, the gray shape of a wreck emerged from the mist. She ran ahead and read the characters on the stern, using a light stick. This really was the *Atagu Maru*. Her father's ship. It was more or less intact. Seventeen years was young for a wreck in the Wind's Teeth. The ship lay heeled over on its starboard side, its keel half-buried in the sand, its deck tilted upward at a steep angle. The masts and yards were naked, stripped of every last rope and sail. Every piece of hardware and scrap of metal on the ship had been removed by scavenging Gublins. Two of the middle masts were gone, clearly blasted away by cannon fire. The ship's rudder was shot to pieces too. And there were several cannon-blasted holes in its hull.

"Pirates," Brieze said.

"Our history says there was little of value in this ship when it was found," Zeelak said. "It appears they lost a battle and their treasure was taken." To her surprise, Zeelak and Zeetog offered to help her search. "We have experience at such things," Zeelak said. "And the sooner we find this book, the sooner we can be on our way."

She told them what to look for, as Mizuki had described it to her: a book bound in dark red leather, with no title or writing of any kind on its cover or spine. "The book's owner was an important person. He would have been staying in one of the private cabins at the rear of the ship. The book is most likely there," she said.

They hopped over the rail, walked up the slanting deck, and climbed down the main hatch into a narrow corridor. The Gublins hung behind Brieze, avoiding the light from her glowstick. They didn't need any extra light to see in the dark. She led the way down the corridor to the stern of the ship. In the eerie quiet, the wood under their feet creaked loudly. There were no cobwebs, no mold or rot in the wood. The sterile environment of the Teeth appeared to have preserved the ship perfectly, just as it was the day it sank. She prepared herself to come upon a skeleton or mummified corpse in the dark, but they encountered no bodies.

The long corridor ended in a narrow passageway with four doors, each leading to a private cabin. The doors were all open and unlocked. Some leaned, broken off their hinges.

A quick glance inside the rooms revealed they'd been ransacked. Their contents were strewn about, and empty, smashed-open chests were scattered here and there.

In one of the rooms, a dozen or more books were scattered across the floor.

My father's cabin, I bet, Brieze thought. "I'll take this one," she said. "You search the others."

She found thirteen books in that room, but none of them bound in red leather. And they all had titles printed on their covers and spines. They were books about science and mathematics, the physics of air travel. She glanced through each to make sure none was a journal in disguise, and she rifled through all the pages, checking for any hidden letters Kaishou might have written. She tossed the last book into the pile she'd made and sat down on the small, shelf-like bed, puzzled and disappointed. This *had* to be Kaishou's cabin. She held her glowstick aloft, and her eyes hunted around the shadowy room. "If I were his private journal," she asked, "where would I be?" The wooden bed creaked as she shifted, and the answer came to her. She jumped up off the bed, knelt beside it, and reached in under the thin mattress.

Her searching fingers found a book.

She pulled it out. It was bound in dark red leather. There was no title on its cover or spine.

She forgot to breathe.

She sat on the bed and—gently—opened the book on her knees. The dry leather of its spine cracked. But the pages were in good shape. With trembling fingers, she flipped through them. They were journal entries, written in a precise, neat hand. She could read the Eastern language much better than she could speak it. She flipped to the last entry. It was much shorter and written much less neatly than the others. She had to guess at some of the hastily scrawled characters…

Pirates! Two ships, well [armed?]. *The captain calls for all men to fight. I wish now I had* [studied?] *more swordplay like my brothers.* [My hands?] *are shaking. I will do my best, and hope to make my family proud.*

Brieze turned the page and read the previous entry…

It has been six weeks now, but feels more like six-hundred. I wish I had made some excuse to stay on Footmont, spend the winter there. How wonderful that would have been. I hate that every day, every hour, takes me farther away from her. I want this blasted ship to get to Kyo now, *so I can finish this silly, tedious business of trading and get on the first ship back to the West. My father will not approve of Patentia, but I don't care. I'll leave Kyo and become a farmer if I have to. Grandma Mizuki may be more understanding. How I wish this voyage were over! I can't even* think *about how long it will be until I see her again. If I did, it would drive me mad.*

Brieze flipped to a new entry, and then to another. There was more, much more, about her mother. It appeared that everything her mother had said was true about how she and Kaishou had met, the time they spent together, their feelings for each other. Kaishou's prose grew quite purple and flowery. He even wrote poems—very bad poems—about her mother. One of them was especially passionate. In fact, it was *explicitly* passionate, Brieze discovered as she read.

"Eww!" she shut the book with a snap.

But she hugged it to her chest. She stood up, and she felt strange to herself. Lighter, shakier, insubstantial. It was as if she wasn't really there, wasn't really *real*. She felt like she might be someone else, someone other than herself. Her father had been a good man. He'd loved her mother. He'd died bravely, fighting pirates. Such a different story than the one she'd told herself over and over again. Her mother had told the truth, and it was she herself who'd made up the lies.

If she had been wrong about this most fundamental part of herself—the beginning—what else about herself had she gotten wrong? What other lies had she told herself? What if she was not the person she thought she was at all?

Who *was* she, really?

The answer just might be that she could be anybody. Anybody at all. Anybody she wanted to be.

The Gublins, searching the cabin next door, were startled by a strange sound. They looked up. It was a sound that had never been heard before in that desolate place, and it would never be heard again. It was the sound of a girl laughing.

They hurried to investigate and met Brieze leaving the cabin, still hugging the book to her chest.

"You found it?" Zeelak asked.

She nodded.

"And it contains the valuable information you were seeking?"

"Beyond price," she grinned, stashing the book in her pack.

✳ ✳ ✳

There by the wreck of the *Atagu Maru*, Zeetog took leave of them to continue his journey west. He clasped hands with Zeelak. Then, to Brieze's surprise, he offered his hand to her.

"I am sorry for what my cousin did to you," he said.

She took his hand. "Thank you."

"I wish you had known him when he was younger. He was kinder then. And not so...damaged."

"I'm sorry I didn't. And I'm sorry for your loss."

Zeetog shouldered his pack and marched away. Soon, the mist swallowed him up.

"Come," Zeelak said, shouldering his own pack. "We have a long walk back."

The three-day walk was a tedious, grueling blur. Zeelak set an even faster pace than before, fretting about the time he was losing. Brieze, anxious to leave the underworld behind and get back to her ship, to return to Kyo with her important news, did her best to keep up. She slogged through the sand behind him, using him to block the wind and stinging grains when she could. They slept only a few hours each night. They ate little, talked less.

When they reached her old campsite and Brieze saw the remains of her fire, her rope still dangling there at the base of the tooth, she felt almost as relieved and grateful as if she had returned to her own bedroom back in the wizard's house. She gave the rope several strong tugs to make sure it was still secure. It was.

She and Zeelak clasped hands.

"We are no longer bound," he said. "I wish you safe traveling."

"Thank you," she said, and faltered, trying to think of something appropriate to say. "It was a pleasure to meet you." There was a silence, and she realized he was waiting for something. "Oh..." she said, remembering. She unpinned the medallion from her jacket and handed it to him. "As we agreed."

He unslung his pack and stashed the medallion in it.

"I've never met a live human before," he said. "It was... interesting."

"It definitely was."

He slung his pack onto his back, turned, and marched away. But before the mist swallowed him up completely, he turned and called out, "Be careful in the world above, silly human, flying around in those flimsy airships! I don't want to come across your bones down here one day!"

Brieze grinned. "I will!"

He disappeared into the fog.

✳   ✳   ✳

She ate the last of her food and lay down to get some sleep and build up some energy for the climb back to the *De-*

vious. She slept Gublin-style, worming her way into the sand and using her pack for a pillow. She felt more like some creature from the underworld than a human being, stiff and sand-encrusted, dry-skinned and leathery. She could barely remember the look and feel of a clear blue sky. Exhausted, she fell asleep faster and slumbered longer than she'd expected to.

When she woke, the feeble, mist-shrouded sun glimmered high in the sky. She stood up and stretched. She pinched the sand from her nostrils. She felt good. The food and rest had done her well. Her body was eager for the climb, eager to be back in its own world, to feel the touch of cold, grit-free wind. She strapped on her climbing cleats and pulled on her gloves. She tied the end of the rope to her pack so she could pull it up after her.

The climb was easier than she expected. Without the pack on her back, she felt light as a feather to herself. And the week of walking with that heavy pack had toughened up her muscles. Her feet found good foot holds and the spiked cleats bit and held tight to the rock. When she reached the little ledge at the halfway point she didn't feel the need to rest, but she stopped there anyway. The sun shone brighter and the fog had thinned. Her heart beat with the anticipation of seeing the *real* sky again. And the *Devious*! She hadn't realized how attached she'd become to her slippery little ship, how much she missed it.

When she finally poked her head up above the big ledge where the *Devious* was anchored, she saw something strange.

A pair of high, well-worn and scuffed black boots stood

right in front of her.

Several more pairs of boots stood around the first pair.

The boots were attached to legs, and the legs were attached to men.

Rough hands seized her and pulled her over the ledge.

Even caught completely off-guard like that, after a hard climb, she put up a good fight. She twisted and clawed and kicked. She saw a knee in front of her and lashed out at it with a fist, putting as much force behind the punch as she could. It felt as if her knuckles shattered against the kneecap, but the man screamed as the leg bent slightly backwards—the wrong way.

"Subdue her you dogs!" a deep voice shouted. "Break an arm if you have to."

There were too many of them. They pinned her arms and legs, knelt on her back, until she squirmed helplessly. When she finally gave up and went slack, they hauled her to her feet, twisting her arms behind her back.

The leader stepped forward and looked her up and down.

He looked at her like he couldn't believe his eyes. His mouth dropped open and he blinked confusedly. She was clearly not what he'd expected to see.

He ran a hand through his bristly, close-cropped white hair. Then, slowly, a malicious grin spread across his harsh and wind-burned face. The thick white scar that ran from the base of his left ear to the corner of his mouth twisted over the deep furrows of his cheek. White teeth gleamed. The grin erupted into a laugh—the long, loud laugh of a man who can't believe his sudden good luck!

The man was Cutbartus Scud, former admiral of the royal fleet, now a traitor, a wanted man in exile. He'd started a war with the Gublins behind the king's back, then tried to discredit the king and take power for himself. But he'd failed, thanks to Brieze and Tak's interference and testimony at court.

The last time he and Brieze met face-to-face, he tried to kill her.

"By all the clouds and currents!" Scud said. "When we saw someone had discovered our little cave here, and appeared to be using it as a base, we had to stick around to see who it was. You are the *last* person I expected to see come climbing up that rope, Missy. What are you doing nosing about the Wind's Teeth in winter? Up to something interesting, I bet."

Her shoulders felt like they were going to pop out of their sockets as Scud's men cruelly twisted her arms. She winced, but looked him straight in the eye with her chin up. "I'm on a geological expedition," she said.

She wasn't a good liar, especially not when put on the spot.

"Geological expedition, huh? Anybody with you?"

"Just my father and a few of his men. They should be up here any minute."

This lie was slightly more convincing, at least to Scud's men. They stepped back from the ledge, put their hands on their sword or dagger hilts, and looked anxiously at him. The men twisting her arms relaxed their grip. The wizard Radolphus of Spire was a powerful man. At the siege of Selestria, he'd single-handedly defeated an entire Gublin army. Even if he wasn't really about to climb up that rope and leap among them, even if he was in fact very far away, still, mistreating his apprentice daughter was a dangerous thing to do.

But Scud never shied away from dangerous things, especially when his ego was involved.

"Bullshit!" he spat. "We've checked out your ship. It's a very interesting ship, by the way. It only has enough supplies for one. Ralston!" he called to one of his men. "Stick your head out over the ledge, give that rope a good tug and see if anybody else is climbing up here."

Ralston looked unhappy about being the one chosen to stick his head out and possibly confront an angry wizard, but he did as he was told. "Can't see anyone climbing up here, but it's pretty foggy down there. Don't feel anybody on the rope," he was pulling it up hand over hand. "Wait! There's something on it. Feels too light for a person."

"Haul it up here," Scud ordered. To Brieze he said, "Anybody who's anybody knows all the wizards are at their summit. There's a wizard's war brewing over this business with the Dragonlord, or my nose has never sniffed the wind before. Your father is far away from here, and preoccupied." He drew a dagger from his belt. It had a well-worn wooden grip and a bright, sharp-looking blade. He lay the tip of the blade against Brieze's throat. "Now," he said. "Why don't you tell me what you're *really* doing here?"

She swallowed. The skin of her throat pulsed against the edge of the blade. She took a deep breath, and she lied better this time. She knew that all good lies had a grain of truth in them. "I was hunting treasure," she said. "In an old wreck."

Scud chewed on this. "Find any?"

"No. The wreck was already scavenged by Gublins when I got there."

"Huh. We'll see about that."

Ralston had hauled her pack up. Scud ordered him to empty it. There wasn't much there. A blanket. An empty water bottle. Some tools and toiletries. A fair amount of sand. And an old book with a cracked red leather cover.

"Now *that* is interesting," Scud sheathed his dagger. "Hand me that book."

Ralston handed it to him. He flipped through the pages. Some of his men crowded around to read over his shoulder. "This is all in Eastern gibberish," he said. "What is it?"

"Nothing," she said. "Just some light reading I brought to pass the time."

Scud snorted. She could see the thoughts churning behind his stormcloud-gray eyes as he glanced back and forth between her and the book. He was a smart man, and he guessed near enough to the truth.

"Wizards don't give a rat's ass about treasure," he said. "No wizard would risk his life in the Teeth for silver or gold. But *knowledge*, now that is something wizards value above all else! Something a young wizard would brave the Teeth in winter for." Scud snapped the book shut. "This old thing obviously came from down there, from one of the wrecks. *This* is the treasure you were seeking. There's some powerful knowledge in this book, I'm guessing." He tossed it to one of the men behind him. "Have one of our Eastern friends give that a read when we get a chance. There's something in it we might find extremely useful, I warrant."

Brieze faked a shrug. "You can have it. I don't care. I've read it." She put up a good front, but she was sick inside. She'd risked so much to find her father's journal. *A book is just a thing,* she reminded herself. *What's important is the information in it. And I have that. They can't take that away from me.* She consoled herself with the thought of one of Scud's friends poring over Kaishou Fujiwara's purple prose and bad poetry, looking for arcane secret knowledge.

"Now Missy," Scud said, grinning. "What are we going to do with *you?*"

NINETEEN

Tak fretted on the trip to No-Man's Crag, but not about their lack of water or the fact they'd soon be wandering around a town full of pirates trying to get some. He fretted about the vision he had of his father. He worried about what it might mean. He kept forgetting to keep an eye on the sail, so that when the wind shifted, the sail would have to flutter and flap loudly for attention before he noticed and adjusted the trim. And there was one other thing that was bothering Tak, too. Finally, he couldn't stand keeping his thoughts to himself any more. He called to Jon. "Can you come here? I need to ask you something."

Jon sat sullenly in the bow of the *Arrow*, wrapped in his cloak, hunched against the cold. The puffs of his breath fogged on the wind like steam from a simmering pot. He was still angry about the incident in The Wind's Teeth. He hadn't spoken the past few days. He stared warily at the Teeth, which glimmered off in the distance directly east as the boys flew north to find their way around them. But the worry in Tak's voice prodded him to stand up with a sigh and make his way aft, climbing over the thwart benches. He plopped down in the stern next to Tak and shrugged to say, *"What?"*

Tak told him about seeing his father standing in the bow of the *Arrow*. About how his father seemed surprised to be there. About his sweat-soaked nightshirt and wild red eyes. About the look of warning he gave. Jon frowned as Tak told the story.

"What do you think it means?" Tak asked.

Jon considered for a while, chewing the beard under his lower lip. "Well," he finally said. "It's not good."

Tak had been dreading that answer. "Do you think he's dead?"

Jon shrugged. "Could be. Or could be he's hovering between this world and the next. Or could be you're starting to lose your mind. Ever had visions before?"

Tak told him about the ghosts of dead Gublins that haunted him after the siege of Selestria.

"Hmmmm…" Jon said.

"What?"

"Sounds like your mind's been a little lost already."

"Thanks."

Jon leaned back and sighed. "Some people have visions, or dreams, or even strong feelings, like premonitions, and they turn out to be true."

"Yeah…?"

"But mostly they don't."

They were quiet for a while, their breath steaming on the wind.

"I hope mine don't," Tak said. "Because for the past couple days, I've also had the awful feeling something bad has happened to Brieze."

"Oh," Jon said. "I bet *that's* true. Wizards are always in some kind of trouble or other."

Tak gritted his teeth and leaned forward as if he could make the *Arrow* fly faster with the force of his will. "We need to get water as quick as we can," he said. "And find her."

EPILOGUE

Admiral Adamus Strake, former captain of the flagship *Dragonbane*, sat chained up in the dark. He sat on a cold stone floor with this knees drawn up to his chest. He circled his arms around his knees and rested his chin on them. He rocked back and forth and muttered to himself. "You can do it," he said. "Just a few more days old boy. Stick with it."

A heavy iron door swung open, its rusty metal hinges grinding. Two guards stepped into the room. One carried a tray of food, the other a small torch, which he held aloft. The torch revealed a cave-like chamber, crudely carved from the rock. Sets of chains and manacles were bolted to the stone walls at regular intervals. The room was designed to hold many men, but at the moment Strake was the only oc-cupant. A heavy iron manacle circled his right ankle. His hands were free, and he raised them to shield his eyes against the torchlight, squinting and blinking and cursing at the guards.

His hair had grown long and ratty, his beard bushy and wild. The blue coat of his admiral's uniform was rumpled and ripped, its seams fraying. His once white breeches were so stained with grime that they were no longer any identifiable color. They had taken his boots. His feet were bare and filthy. His toenails…well, best not to describe those.

The one guard set down the tray of food. He lit a small candle and placed it on the tray. Then the guards left, pulling the door closed behind them. It closed with an iron clang that echoed in the room.

Strake gazed at the little flickering candle. That was different. And then he realized why. Instead of the usual slop they tried to make him eat, there was a steaming bowl of savory chicken stew on the tray. He took a big breath, taking in the scent of onions and herbs, of tender meat and carrots and potatoes. He groaned. His mouth watered. And instead of the chipped wooden cup of stale water, there was a glass carafe of wine! Real, honest-to-goodness ruby-red wine, beckoning to him with the scent of grapes. And there was a glass goblet. And a folded linen napkin. And a silver spoon.

"Damn you!" Strake shouted hoarsely.

His stomach rumbled desperately, frantically. His body begged him to eat.

He crawled on his hands and knees over to the tray. He was weak, and his arms trembled with the effort. The chain of his manacle clinked.

He picked up the bowl of stew. Savored the heavenly scent.

He summoned up all his strength and hurled the bowl across the room.

The carafe of wine followed. It shattered against the stone wall.

The tray and candle followed that. The candle went out. The room went dark again.

Strake made a sound like a little sob. "Good job, old boy," he said in a shaky voice. "Stick with it. Not much longer." He crawled feebly back to his former spot, folded up his knees, wrapped his arms around them, rested his head on them, and resumed rocking back and forth.

Someone lit a torch in the corridor outside. It glimmered dimly though the grate in the door. The iron door creaked open again. A man entered. He was no more than a shadowy figure in the dim light that leaked in from the corridor. He was short, very short, and he moved slowly. He carried another tray of wine and chicken stew. Strake smelled it. The man set it down in the dark, just out of reach. "I hate seeing you suffer like this," he said with a sigh. "Won't you please eat?" He had the voice of a gentle, kindly old man. It was the voice Strake heard in his head the day the dragons destroyed his ship and killed his crew.

"Just let me die," Strake said.

"Why?"

"I'm a traitor to my people. I let you have everything I know about Spire's fleet and our air defenses."

"Is that all?" the old man said. "You shouldn't trouble yourself about that. You couldn't have prevented me from entering your mind and taking what I wanted. No one can. You'd have to have years of training and mental discipline to even try."

"You destroyed my ship. Killed my crew."

"Technically, my dragons did that. I just helped them a

little. And you provoked them you know. They would have passed you by."

"That was the second time."

"Second time for what?"

"Second time I lost my ship and entire crew. In the space of a few months."

"Heavens! That is unfortunate. I'm terribly sorry."

"I'm cursed. I'll never command a ship again. Never fly again. It's best that I just die."

"You're not cursed. There is no such thing as curses. You're just extremely unlucky."

"Cursed. Unlucky. What's the difference? What were your dragons even doing there anyway, on the other side of the world?"

There was a pause. Strake sensed the old man smiling in the dark.

"I would love to tell you," he said. "But I'm afraid information flows only one way in this relationship"

An idea came to Strake. Or at least the fuzzy beginnings of an idea. Something more useful he could do than starve himself to death. "Tell me," he said. "And I'll eat."

There was another pause. Strake sensed the old man's smile broadening. "You have the most fascinatingly stubborn mind," he said. "A real iron will. I've encountered few like it. There are parts of your mind even *I* can't get into."

"Do we have a deal?"

The old man chuckled. "I suppose there's no harm in telling you. Do you swear, on your honor as an admiral, that you will eat?"

"I swear."

"Very well. My dragons were spying. I can enter their minds, see through their eyes, direct their movements. We had been spying on the Kingdom of Frost, and we were on our way to the Kingdom of Spire to do the same thing."

"Why were you spying?"

The old man laughed. "That is an entirely different question, admiral, and not part of our deal." He scooted the tray closer to Strake. "Now eat."

Strake picked up the bowl of stew with trembling hands. He didn't bother with the spoon. He brought it up to his lips, tilted it back, and guzzled from it. He groaned with ecstasy, with relief. He'd never tasted anything so perfectly wonderful in all his life. Stew dribbled down his beard onto his blue admiral's coat.

"Wine?" the old man asked.

"Please," Strake said with tears in his eyes, wiping his lips with a sleeve.

THE SKY RIDERS OF ETHERIUM

Continues in…

The Dragonlord's Apprentice

The adventures Brieze and Tak begin in *The Wizard's Daughter* continue and conclude in Minerd's next book, *The Dragonlord's Apprentice*.

After capturing Brieze in The Wind's Teeth, the pirate Cutbartus Scud sells her as a slave to the Dragonlord, a renegade wizard with the power to control and alter minds. The Dragonlord locks away many of Brieze's "inconvenient" memories so she can better serve as an apprentice. As she adjusts to her new life in the Dragonlord's realm, but plots an escape, she meets someone with knowledge about the disappearance of her father. There is just one problem. She no longer remembers anything about her father, or why she journeyed to the East in the first place.

As Tak searches for Brieze, he runs into Scud in the pirate town of Port Roil. Enraged that Scud sold Brieze as a slave, and goaded by his taunts, Tak challenges him to a duel. To the death.

For more details and information,
visit www.SilverLeafBooks.com

ABOUT THE AUTHOR

AUTHOR PHOTOGRAPH BY HEATHER LEE

Jeff Minerd thought he stopped writing fiction a long time ago until the story for *The Sky Riders of Etherium* came to him not in a dream, but after a dream. He is grateful for that, and for the opportunity to explore the world of Etherium and entertain others with what he finds there.

Minerd has a son, Noah, who is also a writer and avid reader. Minerd hopes to one day place in the top ten—or maybe even top 5—of Noah's favorite authors. But the competition is pretty stiff.

In a previous lifetime, Minerd published short fiction in literary journals, where one of his stories won the F. Scott Fitzgerald short story contest. More recently, Minerd has worked as a science and medical writer for publications and organizations including the National Institutes of Health, *MedPage Today*, *The Futurist* magazine, and the *Scientist* magazine.

Minerd lives in Rochester, NY.

www.JeffMinerd.com

CPSIA information can be obtained
at www.ICGtesting.com
Printed in the USA
BVHW031744301119
565253BV00001B/32/P

9 781609 752279